Kate Elizabeth Clark

The Dominant Seventh

A Musical Story

Kate Elizabeth Clark

The Dominant Seventh
A Musical Story

ISBN/EAN: 9783743399495

Manufactured in Europe, USA, Canada, Australia, Japa

Cover: Foto ©Andreas Hilbeck / pixelio.de

Manufactured and distributed by brebook publishing software (www.brebook.com)

Kate Elizabeth Clark

The Dominant Seventh

THE

DOMINANT SEVENTH

A MUSICAL STORY

BY

KATE ELIZABETH CLARK

NEW YORK
D. APPLETON AND COMPANY
1890

PRELUDE.

"OUR existence in life is a continued alternating of desires and gratifications. The will is forever wanting, and it strives continually to gratify its wants. We really know but two states while in the body—the state of want and the state of satisfaction; the conditions of desire and gratification. Analogous to this, music has but two leading chords, from which all others are derived. These are the tonic chord and the dominant chord of the seventh. The first is a chord of rest and calmness, the second is a chord of unrest, of longing and striving. Music is a continued succession of these two chords, and in this is represented our never-ceasing desires as followed by gratification. Thus the composer reveals the inmost condition of our souls ; he speaks the greatest truth, and speaks it in a language which reason comprehends not, but a language which is understood alike by all men the world over."—SCHOPENHAUER.

THE DOMINANT SEVENTH.

CHAPTER I.

"THAT first violin iss sick once more ahgén," said Karl Klinder, pushing aside the mahogany-colored portière at the door of the McChesneys' music-room, where an amateur club met for weekly practice.

He spoke with the careful accent and precise pronunciation that mark the ambitious German. who desires to be considered a true American citizen. A language, however, being—like beauty—more satisfactory as an inheritance than as an acquisition, and requiring, moreover, for its perfect development abstinence from all demoralizing influences, it is not surprising that the worthy Karl, who rendered faithful homage to the beer-garden and the New York Musicians' Protective Union, should still remain to attentive ears, as well as observant eyes, a German citizen. In view of his announcement, made with Teutonic gravity and a quizzical glance over the top of his spectacles, he

had dispensed with the small formality of an evening greeting. No one, apparently, noticed the
omission.

"Bless me! no; it's impossible—that's the
sixth violinist who has failed us this year! Where
can we find a seventh at this late hour—everything
ready for the concert. We ought to get a *dominant
seventh* this time" (Karl Klinder gave two or three .
little appreciative nods) " in order to have any success at all. Where, where shall we find him?
Well, well!"

Mr. McChesney, who had begun with consider-
ably energy, added the last two words in a waver-
ing tone of resignation. He had come forward as
he spoke, carrying his viola in his hand. He had
just taken it from an antique Flemish cabinet, or
rather cupboard, which stood at one end of the
room and seemed to frown in dignified protest at
the frivolity of an airily draped French window at
the other. In his surprise Mr. McChesney left
the wide doors swinging open to their full extent,
thus revealing a number of musical instruments
resting against a dark-green-cloth background.
Here were a guitar, a banjo, an old-fashioned lute
with its faded blue ribbon, a silver flute, a clari-
net, a cornet, and two violoncellos—one of the long
Stradivarius pattern, like that which once belonged
to Mara, and the other an amber-colored Foster
violoncello of the elegant Amati outline. This

violoncello had a mellow, powerful tone, and was the special delight of Karl Klinder, who made use of it upon some rare occasions when particular depth of feeling was demanded in his solos. On the three shelves below this assortment slept in their coffin-like boxes some valuable violins—a wonderful Amati; a Gaspar di Salo, with its deep brown varnish and its S S holes, straight, well cut, and parallel; an early Antoine Stradivarius, its warm, yellowish varnish still holding the impenetrable secret of its composition; a Joseph Guarnerius, gently arched and daintily curved; a Gagliano; a Bergonzi; and one of our modern but hardly less sweet Gemünders. These violins and other instruments in the Flemish cupboard formed but a small part of his collection, which embraced many examples of ancient instruments, both wind and stringed, and was especially rich in the fine inlaid work and richly carved cases of the eighteenth century makers. It was a collection known to all connoisseurs as unique and almost priceless in value.

Hugh McChesney had certainly made fairly good use of his wealth and leisure during the thirty years that had elapsed since his Harvard College days. The collection of musical instruments was not the only evidence of his dilettanteism; his musical library was replete with those stained and time-worn MSS. in which the great musicians

had stored their immortal thoughts; his small,
well-lighted gallery was hung with excellent examples of different schools of painting; and his long,
low library, with its stained-glass windows and
book-lined walls, revealed, even to the casual observer who glanced along the crowded shelves, a
man of liberal views as well as a man of refined
and even æsthetic tastes. He might best be described perhaps to a musician by the instrument
he preferred—the viola; he was mild, though
firm, and somewhat inclined to melancholy, with
certain tendencies to timidity. Though not self-
assertive in the least, he conveyed to those who
knew him well an impression of reserved power, an
impression which they seldom had the satisfaction
of seeing justified. The atmosphere always sur-
rounding him was that of kindness; children
and animals were particularly attracted to him;
men liked him unless they were coarse natured,
when his refinement and purity of thought acted
upon them paradoxically like a counter-irritant;
women adored him with that calm friendliness
and confidence which generally precludes the pos-
sibility of deeper emotion. He was squarely and
sturdily built, somewhat muscular, and the distinguishing feature of his face was a pair of liquid
brown eyes whose darkness seemed intensified by
the iron-gray hair and mustache. He dressed
with more regard to comfort than to fashion, for

he believed that clothes were made for man rather than man for clothes. He stood in the center of the room, and, still facing Karl Klinder, anxiously asked :

" But what is to become of our quartet? The concert is to come off next week. The tickets are all sold. And to bring in, at the last moment, a professional whose theories in regard to the quartet may be entirely different from ours, whose interpretation we may be compelled to follow after we have studied our own so carefully—why, bless me, it's not to be thought of! Here we have spent weeks of labor in acquiring the happy medium between the old classical interpretation and the new Wagnerian intensity of emotional expression. What can be done? The situation is—is—well—really it is exasperating. Will he not be able to come to another rehearsal if not to this one?"

Karl Klinder shook his bullet head dubiously, and, grasping his 'cello tenderly by the neck, proceeded to carry it to a safe corner of the music-room, where he set it down without removing its outer cover of waterproof or its inner dress of soft green flannel. Then he deposited himself with vigor in a straight, high-backed chair, and remarked deliberately :

" He hass shills ahgén. He gomplains wit them some time since hlately."

" Diable ! Peste soit d'l'ignorant!" broke in a

voice from near the piano where a man stood alternately striking A and E while he tuned his violin. "If he has malaria there is little chance of his regeneration in time for our concert. It is the one thing that blows away all sense of duty and propriety and leaves a man one vast sickly interrogation point. As for his music, let us give it up at once. He could only play Schumann's 'Why' or that antique obituary-canvas-sampler, Mendelssohn's 'Resignation.'"

"Perhaps if you had a tiny soupçon of malaria, yourself, Emil, your interpretation of certain musical movements might be better," said Philip McChesney, a tall, dark-eyed young man, leaning over the end of the grand piano.

"Eh, bien! I know you don't altogether like my sentiment in the andantes, adagios, and largos of our symphonies and sonatas, but it is because I express in them a natural reaction against this New Jersey malarial atmosphere—sentimentally damp or dam-p-dly sentimental. Why *do* you live here at all? Was New Jersey *ever* celebrated for anything but peaches and mosquitoes?"

"Gently, gently, Emil," interrupted Philip McChesney; "Jersey has one other merit—it gives you shelter from a Russian prison. We don't object to your criticism, but give the devil his due. And permit me to doubt, mon ami, whether, even if you should have malaria, you would then be able to wail with proper feeling, or to bring out delicately any phrase of deep heart-longing, unless it might be some expression of your desire to see the Czar biting the dust. But give you a movement where you can represent a dance of Nihilists around a toppling palace—interjections of dynamite ad libitum—there and then you can outrival Remenyi's most frenzied improvisations. Your playing is all very well in Rubinstein and Tschaikowsky, but not *quite* the thing in a Beethoven adagio. Perhaps it's just as well though to have a revolutionary spirit among us, otherwise we steady-going citizens might become threads of attenuated sweetness. By a wise dispensation of Providence enters Kalinski—anarchy, dismay, colored fire, death to rulers!"

"You seem to measure your wit by rule, mon enfant," said Emil quickly.

"No, by rote; the pen of history is my divining-rod," answered Philip, pressing his hand to his heart and bowing with exaggerated courtesy.

"Votre tres-humble serviteur, monsieur," said Emil, straightening himself and giving a military salute with his violin.

The two men presented a striking contrast. Emil Kalinski was undersized, with long body, short legs, large head, dark bushy whiskers parted in the middle and brushed to stand out from the face. He had, moreover, a large mouth with full red lips which ordinarily remained slightly open over gleaming and rather projecting teeth. Philip McChesney, on the contrary, was built like his father, with the exception of being taller and more slender. He had, too, a longer nose and brighter eyes and possessed that greater elasticity and hopefulness of bearing that usually distinguishes youth from middle age. His face was refined and thoughtful and his every movement graceful. Equally striking was the mental contrast between these two men. Emil, born in Russia and accustomed during his youth to the morbid atmosphere of secret sympathy with Nihilism, educated in France and imbued there with the strongest communistic sentiments, displayed in his conversation a curious mixture of dogged bitterness, reserve, and suspicion, and sullen egotism, but thinly veiled by a superficial polish and vivacity. Philip was the soul of frankness and honor and good fellowship, and, inheriting from his mother a keen sense of humor, he was inclined to look at the cheerful side of existence. His greatest fault was an easy-going disposition that led him to put himself on terms of comradeship with all varieties of men. Between him and Kalinski existed a warm friendship; although indeed a suspicion now and then crossed Philip's mind that Kalinski had not an overkeen sense of honor and that he might be capable under temptation of sinking virtue in self-interest. Nevertheless, he tried to thrust away such unwelcome thoughts even when a chance remark, like a ray of light let suddenly into a darkened room, revealed the unwelcome possibilities of Kalinski's nature.

While Philip and Emil continued their passage at arms by the piano, Mr. McChesney and Karl Klinder were carrying on a serious discussion, which ended when Mr. McChesney turned to Philip, and said :

" Well, my son, there is no way out of the present difficulty but for you to work up this violin part. By practicing night and day you may be able to do it. If it were not for these private theatricals, nonsensical germans, and the superfluity of pretty girls here, you might have been a fine violinist by this time. At any rate, try the part. You have heard it often enough to have a right conception of it."

"All right, for once, paternus," answered Philip, smoothing a slight wrinkle in the shoulder of his well-fitting dress-coat, and then conveying the white carnation from his button-hole to a vase of cameo-glass filled with roses. " I will give my valuable aid until the carriage comes at half-past nine o'clock. Aux armes, citoyens !

Gather the notes in while ye may,
Old Time is still a-flying."

Philip seized his violin as he spoke and compelled the unoffending instrument to execute a series of discordant shrieks in harmony with the feelings of his listeners. After this ebullition he sat down quietly to prepare for the serious work before him.

The rehearsal proceeded fairly for a time. They were playing Beethoven's E flat major quartet, op. 127. The opening chords, "maestoso," the allegro, even the first part of the noble adagio whose penetrating sweetness and deep feeling touches even an unmusical heart, met with not entirely unworthy treatment at the hands of these enthusiastic amateurs, but alas for the syncopations, the delicate trills, the groups of thirty-second notes that should sway and sigh as lightly as vine leaves on a trellis !

"Quarter of a tone off and scratchy at that," said Mr. McChesney, laying down his viola when Philip struck the high A flat in the closing measures of the andante con moto.

"It *is* a shame to murder such a glorious movement," Philip remarked mournfully. "I *feel* it all. *Why* will not the mind control the muscles?"

"It might if you exercised both sufficiently," said Mr. McChesney grimly.

"I call that mean, paternus, to hit a man when he's already down in his boots. However, I have some coals of fire for Newcastle—I know a man

who, I think, will help us. Go on practicing, and
I will bring him if possible. There is the carriage, now."

Philip seized his carefully preserved carnation,
pinned it again in his button-hole, and went out
of the room.

"But who is it you propose to introduce in
this unceremonious fashion?" Mr. McChesney
called after Philip.

"Oh, *he's* all right," replied Philip, coming
back to the door with his overcoat on. "I heard
him at the De Peysters' in New York last week.
He has come out here to board for the winter, as
he likes quiet. And he'll certainly get enough of
it. Suburban New Jersey towns don't offer alarm-
ing opportunities for hilarious dissipation—mild
sociables, spasmodic teas, church-fairs, and mis-
sionary jug-breakings, with a sprinkling of euchre-
parties and a climax of an occasional german.
Pah!"

Mr. McChesney looked benignantly at his son.
"Philip, my boy, you are a weather-vane. How
long is it since you defended Jersey against Kalinski?"

"Et tu, Socrate! Whether vain or not vain,
at least I'm not a-spire-ing enough to reach your
philosophic height." And Philip hastened off,
leaving his father smiling and shaking his head
at this parting shot.

CHAPTER II.

PHILIP sped on his way with little doubt of the success of his mission. He had a strong belief in the general kindly spirit of musicians toward each other, notwithstanding the fact that they have been so long compelled to appear in public as æsthetic scapegoats for the ill-tempers common to all humanity. Philip had found, like many others who investigate for themselves, that there exists among musicians, particularly the better class of professionals and amateurs, a sympathy whereby they appreciate at once each other's wants and needs, and which renders them sufficiently alive to direful musical possibilities to step forward graciously when awkward gaps are to be filled. It is only the penny-a-liner, so to speak, of the musical world, who plays the part of Jupiter nodding to mortals, and who leaves his petitioner dubious as to his intentions on the appointed evening. Your true, sensitive musical genius will respond if possible to the call of a brother in distress with that gentle courtesy that doubles the obligation while disclaiming any.

Philip's expectations were fully justified. Signor Ferranti was at home and, after listening to Philip's explanation, expressed his willingness to attend the rehearsal. He donned a fur-lined overcoat and slouch hat, under which his yellow face and large black eyes assumed a softer aspect, took his violin, which he told Philip had been presented to him by a well-known connoisseur in Paris and was worth at least five thousand dollars, and without further delay entered the carriage. Conversation flagged; for Philip received but monosyllabic answers to his good-natured questions. The night was clear. There was a full moon. A high wind blew, driving fragments of clouds over the sky—fragments tinged whenever they drifted across the moon with yellow opaline luster. The trees, to which still clung a few withering leaves, like the last faint hopes that cling to the heart of an aged man, took on a blue-gray tint under the pallid light and fitfully swayed to and fro as the carriage rolled up the long winding drive that led up hill to Strathcarron. An irregular stone dwelling crowned the top of the hill, and from the front of this dwelling a magnificent lawn swept cheerfully and expansively away, its gentle slope dotted in summer with beds of brilliant flowers, groups of tropical plants, and well-clipped cedars and pines. A rustic bridge crossed a dashing little stream that ran some distance to the right, and

2

off some distance to the left a trout-pond was half visible under its protecting hedge of willows and low bushes. Ferranti woke from his reverie to remark upon the beauty of the place.

"It is like an old English mansion," said he, noting the turrets at the corners, the high tower rising in the center, and the Doric pillars that supported a generous portico.

"Yes; the main body of the house was built by my grandfather to resemble the early home of his wife, who was an Englishwoman of some rank; but it has received several additions since. The music-room is on the right side of the house, and extends through to another long piazza on the back; and out of the music-room opens a small conservatory which is my sister's special delight. In the music-room we have been fortunate enough to hear some of the best musicians in the world: Ole Bull, Remenyi, Wieniawski, Musin, that best of classic artists Wilhelmj, and any number of the great pianists—Mme. Essipoff, Madeleine Schiller, Joseffy, and our latest American acquisition, Adèle Aus der Ohe. And it is a curious fact that in a private music-room, and surrounded only by the appreciative few, they have generally played with even more fire and feeling than in a public hall."

"That may well be true," answered Ferranti. "The best music I have heard lately was in the

small salon in Paris where Saint Saëns entertains
his music-loving friends."

As they stepped out of the carriage the opening strains of the Gade trio in F major floated
to their ears and seemed to fill the air with spring-
like joyous freshness.

"Who plays the piano?" asked Ferranti
abruptly, taking off his hat.

"My sister Flora," Philip answered. Ferranti
stood still for a moment and, as if unconscious of
a listener, repeated a line from Dante, " Quando
ti giovera dicera io fui." He then turned and
walked slowly to one end of the piazza and stood
motionless, evidently impressed with the beauty of
the scene. In the distance rose the church-spires;
a low range of hills melted into the dark clouds
along the horizon line; here and there lights
gleamed from the windows of the houses below;
and, over all, the moon and clouds threw an ever-
shifting network of light and shade. All was
quiet, domestic, and American, save Ferranti himself who, with his loose long cloak, his bare head,
and his sharp, strong features accentuated by a
sudden flood of moonlight, brought to Philip's
mind flitting visions of Roman senators, Socratic
philosophers, Italian banditti, and Spanish cava-
liers.

As Philip unlocked the door with his latch-
key and stood back to let Ferranti step over the

CHAPTER III.

FEW men of artistic temperament could fail to be affected by the sweet womanliness of Flora McChesney, combined as it was with an almost masculine directness of thought and a swiftness of comprehension that made her one of the most charming companions in the world. To see her hazel eyes gleam with a quick perception of the speaker's coming thought offered an irresistible source of pleasure to men of intellect and taste; and even the taciturn were moved in her presence to express themselves with ease and freedom. She was never called beautiful, save in those rare moments of excitement when a brilliant color lent to her pale face the rosy light of youth. Her features were rather large and not over-finely modeled; but the mouth—that feature for which one is most directly responsible—was sweet and firm. A slender, willowy figure made her appear younger than her twenty-six years. Two peculiarities were always first noted by strangers—one, the mass of fluffy golden hair which crowned a well-shaped head, each hair seemingly endowed with a separate will of its own; the other, the large, flexible hands, with fingers capable of bending backward and forward with equal facility. The size of her hand did not at all disturb Flora McChesney, for this defect was balanced in her eyes by the ease with which in her piano-playing she compassed abnormal stretches and obtained superior orchestral effects. She was a well-read woman, capable of understanding the scientific researches of Lubbock and the lines of thought pursued by Darwin, Huxley, and Spencer, and not above enjoying the insouciance and freshness of some second or even third-rate novels of the day. Indeed, this recreation she held to be a necessity, and considered that any woman of broad culture must know all currents of thought of her time and must comprehend the amusements of the many as well as the interests of the few.

In music she was no less catholic in her tastes; not finding Offenbach and Strauss unbearable because Beethoven and Wagner are sublime, but looking upon them all as ministers of grace who preach not unworthily of that whereof each one knows. This general appreciativeness which did not seem to interfere with the preservation of her high ideals became still more noticeable when one observed her social relations. Hence it was not surprising that her admirers were only limited by the number of her acquaintances. The violinists invariably succumbed audibly or with secret sighs, according to the stability of previous anchorage, to her attractions; while of other admirers might be named, almost at random, a lean flutist, two cellists, both stout and red, a zither artist, a doctor with a good practice, besides three artists, an enthusiastic bibliophile, and a scientific man who wished to add her, as she declared, to his unique collection of butterflies. Few among the musicians, however, had ventured to come to the point of offering their full hearts and empty pockets to a divinity who hedged herself about with an atmosphere of such cold reserve, and who looked upon love as an epidemic : not necessarily fatal.

From the library, across the hall and opposite the music room, Flora listened to the new violinist. She heard his preliminary suggestions in a rich, mellow voice; then the opening chord of E flat, forte ; the light, firm, staccato repetition ; then the dominant seventh, sforzato; so on, as the instruments swept to the tenderly strong allegro. The master spirit gradually made itself manifest, animated the other players, and bent them to its own will. Heavens! what fire and spirit flamed into this new reading! The old interpretation was forgotten. Phrase after phrase came out with new and dramatic meaning. The grand epic force of Beethoven, the concentrated energy with which

he drew from human life its mysterious secrets—
its wild despair, its bitter grief, its tender affection, its ever-springing hope—and brought them
into noble relationship through his divine harmonies, which drop the balm of peace over the
listener's heart, and rise in triumphant majesty
to meet the bending stars, these received from
Ferranti the perfect recognition of a truly musical
soul.

The usual tempo quite forgotten, the players
hurried with repressed excitement through the
staccatos and the swinging triplets of the final
allegro con moto. As with increasing impetu-
osity they reached the end, Flora drew near
the door of the music room and stood there
quietly, her pale face and yellow hair thrown
out in strong relief by the dark velvet folds of
the portière that fell in heavy masses on either
side. She looked straight at Ferranti, and when
the last dominant seventh chord, followed by the
tonic, brought the movement to an end, she said
eagerly :

" That is the way Beethoven would have played
it had he lived to-day, had he been familiar with
our own modern life."

Ferranti lifted his head, lowered his violin,
and gazed at her dreamily, as if bringing himself back with difficulty to the world of real
life.

" Yes, that is the way, I think."

The others sat as though stupefied by their own unexpected power. Their eyes were fixed upon the sallow, impassive face, which bore no trace of emotion. Mr. McChesney held out his hand and warmly shook that of the violinist. Karl Klinder wiped his spectacles. Kalinski mopped his forehead excitedly.

" Is there anything more? " said Ferranti, rising. Mr. McChesney rose also.

" Well, perhaps not. There was a sonata for piano and violin on our programme, but—" And he hesitated.

Flora came forward. " Oh, we must play it, father." A bright red spot came to either cheek as she began to look for the music.

" What is it? " said Ferranti. " Ah, a Raff sonata, that ' Fünfte Grösste,' a fifth monument to his industry—dry bones that rattle correctly enough in obedience to the showman's jerking-string. But to be just, some of Raff's compositions are lovely; it is only when he insists on working a poor idea through forty pages of fugal and contrapuntal variations that he becomes so tiresome. Do you know the suite opus 210? That is a charming piece of work."

" Yes," said Flora.

" But whom do you like best of the modern composers? Rubinstein? I thought so. Let us run over one of his sonatas. Which shall it be?"

"The G major I am most familiar with," Flora answered, taking the music from the tall ebony rack by the piano.

Ferranti looked at her with an expression of surprise ; then, as if deterred by some inward thought from expressing any objection, he took the music from her hand and put it slowly upon the stand before him.

In spite of her own strong will, which made her cling to her wonted interpretation of the sonata, Flora was soon overpowered by the magnetism of Ferranti. Like the players in the quartet, she lost her own individuality and followed the violinist's thought. By that wonderful sympathy which had always been the distinguishing characteristic of her accompaniments, she grasped each phrase almost before its enunciation by the violin ; while her own prominent passages came out with startling likeness to the violin tones, rippling, dancing, leaping from the quivering instrument in Ferranti's hands. A moment's pause after the scherzo : another after the brief adagio that opens the finale : then they dash into that free and joyous strain which forms the principal motif of the last movement :

Flora shivered as she began the strain.

The violin slid into the long D that begins the violin accompaniment, and the piano took up the motif. Flora glanced up in astonishment at Ferranti, half turned her head apprehensively, and lost for a moment the rhythm. More and more nervously she moved her long fingers over the sixths, octaves, and elusive arpeggios of the difficult accompaniment. Now the rich bass tones of the piano gave out the motif transferred to the key of B flat, now the violin followed; now fugally

both intertwined; now through the key of C minor
the motif moved with growing pathos; then in D
minor it breathed out its meaning with swelling,
sorrowful intensity, like a thought of remembered
happiness that fills the aching heart with tears.
Flora had grown gradually paler, and at the climax of the musical emotion—the high forte F of
the violin—she let her hands fall upon the keys
with a crashing discord; sprang up, dashed her
right hand into the air as against some repellent
object, and gave at the same time a piercing
shriek. Her father ran to the piano and grasped
her by the arm, while she struggled and cried
out:

"Oh! send her away! What is she here for?
Who is she?" and she looked around the room
with dazed eyes.

"No one is here, my child," said Mr. McChesney gently.

"But I saw a terrible face. I felt a thrill of
horror when I began that movement, as if something dreadful were about to happen; and while
we played that last passage I felt a presence beside
me. I looked up and there was that face—a
woman's face, pale and haggard, with wild, star-
ing eyes and black hair falling in straggling locks
upon the forehead and over the shoulders. The
eyes were glittering with fury, and a hand was
raised to strike me. Merciful Heavens! I was so

frightened. Who was it? What could it have
been?" And she clung trembling to her father's
arm.

"Nothing, I imagine, but nervousness and a
vivid imagination," said her father, patting her
quietly on the shoulder with his disengaged hand.
"We have had too much music to-night, perhaps.
You had better sit down a while," directing her
unsteady movements to a large brown velvet arm-
chair near the door.

Flora sank into the chair and threw her head
back, half-closing her eyes. At this moment the
old housekeeper, Flora's former nurse, a Scotch-
woman by birth and a privileged character by
merit, came rushing in, her wide cap-border waving, a flask of smelling-salts in one hand and a
bottle of camphor in the other.

"Ah, my bit bairnie, what have ye noo? I
heard ye scream and I did na ken were ye mur-
dered or no."

Flora put out her hand to grasp that of the
old woman, but her face grew whiter.

"Dinna ye ken she's gaun to faint?" said Maggie to the men, who afforded the usual example in
such cases of masculine intellects struggling to
eliminate the useless factors of logic, law, and
precedent from the problem in view, and to make
$X = $ What to do.

"Bring me some cold water," she continued,

to Mr. McChesney, while she rubbed Flora's hands. He hastened to the dining-room, quickly returned with the water, and, according to Maggie's directions, tried to bathe Flora's forehead. He was awkward, and the water trickled over her face. Karl Klinder, standing ready to be useful, seized Maggie's long, soft, white apron to wipe away the water-drops. " Hoot mon, ye're owre free wi' what's no' yer ain," said she abruptly; for no anxiety could make Maggie entirely forgetful of her personal dignity.

"It is a vay I haf when dhere iss necessity," Karl answered calmly, nevertheless substituting his own red silk handkerchief for the well-protected apron.

Under Maggie's energetic ministrations Flora soon recovered consciousness. " Where is mamma ? " she asked.

" The mither didna hear ye, bairnie; she's in the faraway room wi the laddies. Do ye feel better noo, dearie ? " And the woman pushed back the wet curls from Flora's forehead.

" Yes, indeed," said Flora sitting up with an evident effort. " Please do not say anything to mamma. And don't make any more fuss over me, anybody, please. I am only a little upset, that is all. It is absurd for me to be nervous." She gave a little hysterical laugh as she observed the three men gazing at her with solemn earnestness;

her father calmly spilling the glass of water, Klinder holding the red silk handkerchief, and Kalinski poising in the air a huge Japanese fan which
he had snatched from its place in the hall. Ferranti alone remained at the farther end of the
room and peering with apparent intentness at the
musical instruments in the Flemish cabinet.

"You really look too funny," she continued;
"I remind myself of Juno, sitting on a cloud
and receiving attentions from the gods."

"Nae, nae, lassie," broke in Maggie; "ye're
mair like a modest blue-bell o' the mountains than
like any o' the auld wights who sit aboon the airth
and ken naething at all about it, savin to crachit
their sels oop wi' their ain selfishness."

"Well, I suppose it is my fate to be always a
'bit lassie' to you, Maggie, and never, never, a
stately Juno." Flora spoke affectionately, and
leaned upon Maggie's arm while she tried to say
good-night with some degree of composure. But
the quivering of her lips and her pallor showed
the effort that it cost her; and her self-possession
was nearly lost when upon saying "Good-night,
Signor Ferranti," he wheeled suddenly about and
flashed from his dark eyes an intense questioning
glance vividly contrasting with his former as-
sumption of indifference. After Flora went out
Mr. McChesney walked up and down the room a
few times, reflectively clasping and unclasping his

hands. At length he stopped near Ferranti and remarked in a rather apologetic tone :

"This is the first evidence of hysterical weakness I have ever seen in my daughter. She is not of the ordinary feminine emotional type; she has unusual self-control. I can not understand such a singular freak. It is really quite puzzling."

Signor Ferranti put down the violin he was examining, and said, somewhat vaguely it seemed to Mr. McChesney: "Positive blondes are generally very susceptible to emotional influence, even though they appear to be self-controlled. Negative blondes, on the contrary, of the ashen type, get credit for much more feeling than they deserve because their narrowness and cunning permits them to hysterically impose upon the average man. It is the occasional decided blonde like your daughter who redeems the petty sins of the whole type." Ferranti spoke in a would-be calm, didactic manner, but his low tone betrayed a vibrating undercurrent of feeling, and his hand trembled as he walked away to put his own violin in its case.

Mr. McChesney, whose mind was thus turned from his daughter's emotional disturbance, had begun already in imagination to prepare a few statistics in regard to the theory that blondes are dying out, and was not overpleased at the retreat of a possibly appreciative listener. He followed Ferranti to the piano, but, seeing him about to

leave, wisely forbore discussion and remarked upon
the beauty of the violin cover. It was of black
velvet, lined and bound with orange satin and embroidered with a lyre in gold thread and a wreath
of passion flowers.

"Evidently a labor of love," was his medita-
tive, rather than interrogative remark.

"Probably, since all art work is a labor of love.
But the best work can be bought. That is the
curse of it," with an amused curl of the lip.
"Good evening," and the signor shook hands
with Mr. McChesney and left before the other oc-
cupants of the room had time to notice his departure.

"His hands were like the hands of a dead
man," Mr. McChesney said. "Bah! can that
foolish child have affected me with her nervousness?"

"Perhaps Signor Ferranti hass also a shill, or
in—indig—nation—how do you call you the stomach trouble?" Klinder suggested mildly but sar-
castically as he tied the waterproof bag over his
'cello.

Kalinski said nothing. He had been greatly
disturbed by the sudden advent of Signor Ferranti. With the keen instinct of jealousy, he fore-
saw a powerful rival. For it was a fact but half
suspected that Kalinski was Flora's most persist-
ent adorer. He knew, indeed, that she cared little

or nothing for him; but although he apparently neither expected nor asked any concession from her, he patiently bided his time and hugged to himself the delusion that one day his devotion would be rewarded. He was swayed by that self-ish passion which considers only its own gratifi-cation and has no regard for the real welfare of its object. Of love in the true meaning of the word he had no conception; so that when Philip attempted one day to convince him that love must be the *mutual* recognition of two souls drawn to each other by an irresistible attraction which ex-cludes the idea of selfishness, Emil Kalinski mere-ly gave Philip in return a superior smile of egotis-tic pessimism, and proceeded at once to expound his own theories:

"Love?" said he, briskly. "What do you know of love more than I? You have one idea of it, and there are others. How many kinds of love are there?—all branches of one thrifty tree. None knows better what love means than Wagner. Are his heroes all alike? Are his heroines alike? Let me remind you—in another's words—of, for in-stance, Senta, 'the human embodiment of that love which is rather a blind, adoring faith than a passion, and which feeds and thrives upon com-plete self-abandonment and sacrifice'; of Elsa, 'a no less passionate love, although not incapable of self-sacrifice, which must instinctively and irre-

sistibly have fuller and yet fuller possession of its
object'; or Kundria, 'the representative of two
antagonistic traits in woman—of feminine love,
ever devoted, self-sacrificing, and hopeful, and of
feminine fascination and seduction, ever baneful,
enervating, and fraught with ruin'; and I might
give a thousand instances to illustrate a poet's
standpoint. As to myself—if I love a woman, she
is mine if I can win her. If she doesn't love me
—well, so much the worse *if* I win her. But I
take the chances of her loving me—it is woman's
nature to love her master. Liberty of love and
love of liberty are my watchwords."

"Rather Mephistophelian," said Philip quietly.
"Ça va," with a shrug. "But your cherished theories will vanish when Love knocks at the door of
your heart.

> Nicht Gut, nicht Gold,
> Noch göttliche Pracht,
> Nicht Haus, nicht Hof,
> Noch herrischer Prunk,
> Nicht Trueber Vertraege,
> Truegender Bund,
> Noch heuchelnder Sitte
> Hartes Gesetz
> Selig in Lust und Leid
> Lässt—die Liebe nur sein."

CHAPTER IV.

IN the interval that elapsed between this rehearsal and the concert, Signor Ferranti visited the McChesneys twice—once to attend a rehearsal, where he played the suite of Raff's selected for the concert instead of the Rubinstein sonata, and once in response to an invitation to dine from Mrs. McChesney. On the latter occasion his melancholy gravity exercised a depressing effect upon the family, especially upon Mrs. McChesney, who, with the curious stupidity which sometimes characterizes a bright woman, insisted upon entertaining a man who did not require to be entertained at all. But in spite of his silence they received the impression that he could be eloquent if necessary, an impression heightened by the gleam of quick interest which now and then lightened his face at a humorous speech from Philip or a noble thought from Flora or her father.

"Hugh?" said Mrs. McChesney to her husband, as they all congregated in the library after Signor Ferranti had gone, "Hugh"—a downward inflection this time—"did you notice anything peculiar about our guest? I do not mean his manners, for he is certainly familiar with the usages of polite society, and I don't mean his silence, although that is disagreeable enough to *me*, I am sure." She continued with a slightly aggrieved air, "I almost hate a man who makes you feel as if he were punctuating your sentences with 'useless,' 'silly,' 'meaningless'; jabbing the stiletto of his logic through your mild aphorisms, and finally holding the whole web of your attempted conversation up to the light of reason, just to show you how thin and slazy it is. And all the time inwardly congratulating himself that *he* doesn't say silly things. I prefer a hundred times that a man should sometimes say a silly thing rather than always appear like Atlas in our old geographies—burdened with the weight of the world."

"Bravo, little mother!" said Philip, putting his arm about his mother's neck. "You will always love your children, that is sure; for they have no warning voice to guard them from saying those airy nothings which a very wise man might endow with a local habitation by dubbing them 'vulgar fractions.' Let me see—something seems amiss there; but they do puzzle the unwary, these airy nothings—silly or subtle according to the nature of the owner. Now, our silly things—"

"Are 'generally silly,'" interrupted Mr. McChesney. "Now, my dear Josephine, perhaps you will let us know what is so peculiarly peculiar about Signor Ferranti."

"Oh! I mean his habit of slowly turning his head in a half-dazed manner when one speaks to him, as if the sound came from far off; and also his habit of looking quickly over his shoulder now and then, as if annoyed by some invisible presence."

"I have noticed the first habit, but it is one so common among literary and musical people that I attribute it to the calm abstraction of genius. The second habit I have not noticed. I have had time to note, though, that Signor Ferranti is a man of unusual culture. This evening, when I showed him some of my books, he handled my 'black letters' and my Aldine and Elzeverian imprints with the tender care that marks a genuine book-lover. He was perfectly fascinated by the Venetian 'De Imitatione,' 1483, and by my Peter Lombard; and he gave me a most interesting account of some fine vellum MSS., breviaries, and psalters in the possession of his uncle at Milan; particularly of an exquisite Flemish 'Book of Hours,' with floriated capitals. His uncle's collection must be valuable and unique. And, my dear, though Signor Ferranti says little, he says enough to show sympathy with the thoughts and interests of others. He is a gentleman and an artist, and entitled to courtesy and recognition

in any society. He is far superior to the young
scions of old families that will not meet him on
terms of social equality."

"Yes," said Philip, "the difference there is decidedly in Ferranti's favor. Brain in his case can
be spelled correctly, but in the case of the others
the 'i' must be left out."

"What do you think, Flora?" continued Mr.
McChesney, after a quiet chuckle at Philip's sally.

Flora glanced up from the book she had not
been reading. "He certainly is a man of great
ability, but to me there is something mysterious
and uncanny about him."

"Well, let us hope you won't *always* see ghosts
when you play with him. A man who can play
the violin as he does *may* have the power of hypnotic suggestion." Philip yawned, and medita-
tively leaned against the mantel-piece while he
continued : "Kalinski does get into a dickens of a
humor sometimes. He evidently hated Ferranti
the other night because he played those Paganini
studies so well ; and when Ferranti did that marvelous 'double-stopping,' Kalinski glared as if he
thought the signor old Janus himself. Kalinski
is quite a decent fellow, on the whole ; but talk of
mystery—he gives me the impression sometimes of
being a sort of suppressed Jack-in-the box who
might at any moment pop up grinning and shaking his rattle of 'Death and Defiance!' to the

whole world. I don't like to be suspicious, but I could mistrust him sooner than I could mistrust our silent Italian."

" Come, come ! we are getting too imaginative," said Mr. McChesney. " That is the trouble with the musically inclined; the emotional nature is apt to overbalance the reasoning powers."

" I am glad our concert is safe," Mrs. McChesney remarked with a sigh of satisfaction. " That is now the main consideration. I can't bear to do a thing at all unless it is done well, especially for charity. I never believe in compelling my friends to listen to a poor performance, even for charity's sake; nor for that matter in any entertainment the results of which are five hundred dollars for expenses and five for charity."

Mrs. McChesney carried out her own theories. In her entertainments given for " The Hospital," " The Old Ladies' Home," and other local charities, she utilized the musical talent of her own family and of her professional friends, who, by reason of her kindly and unbounded hospitality, offered freely their services. Decorations and refreshments were simple and inexpensive, and the entire proceeds of each entertainment were given to the charity in question. For these reasons, and from the fact that tickets were only sold by invitation, it was a foregone conclusion that a concert at the McChesneys would be well attended. This

particular concert proved no exception. Carriages
rolled in rapid succession to the door; group after
group of well-dressed men and women flitted up
the broad stairway lined on either side with huge
ferns, palms, and tropical plants. When the guests
descended and entered the library they received
programmes of unique design from two young
McChesneys, aged respectively eight and ten, both
dressed, to their own delight and as a guarantee of
good behavior, in mediæval troubadour costumes.
The hostess received in the long drawing-room
back of the library. She thus removed the formal,
funereal atmosphere that in general marks a par-
lor concert. The guests quickly distributed themselves according to pleasure; the more sedate went
to the music-room proper, or to the gallery above,
which, crossing one side of the room, afforded
from behind the carved railing surmounted by
busts of musicians good vantage ground for hearing if not for seeing; while those who rejoiced in
the first heyday of youth sought secluded corners
of the conservatory, library, and halls where, un-
disturbed by admonitory frowns, they could in-
dulge in sly flirtations, sibilant whispers, and even
occasional giggles.

The music-room had never looked more invit-
ing. From innumerable lamps and wax candles a
soft light shone through shades of delicate colors.
In the four corners of the room were orange trees

in fruit and bloom, their bases veiled by pots of feathery ferns, their fragrance filling the air with that indescribable scent of purity and loveliness combined, which, in addition to the velvet whiteness of the blossoms, has led the poet to hold the tree as typical of chastity and the maid to hold it sacred to her wedding-day. Along the gallery and along the opposite side of the room, whose plain light-gray surface was broken by the velvet portière and by three recesses containing bronze statues of Bach, Beethoven, and Wagner, were festooned triple ropes of smilax. These festoons were caught up below each bronze bust on the gallery railing and above each statue's head by a cluster of solid-colored chrysanthemums—orange, blood-red, yellow, or crimson—placed against a semicircle of radiating narrow leaves of the common gladiolus. In front of the Flemish cabinet stood a tall vase of bluish-green Satsuma holding a few immense plumy spikes of the brilliant salt-meadow golden-rod; while before the French window clustering branches of the rose-colored wild aster and delicate white eupatorium sprang up to crown the loveliness of a marble wood-nymph who leaned against a rose-veined marble tree-trunk.

Miss McChesney assumed the ever-thankless task of opening the programme. She played Bach's prelude and fugue in C sharp minor—the fugue as delightful as the prelude is uninteresting—and

she received a perfunctory sort of applause due
more to her charming appearance than to interest
in Bach. For it is undeniably and sadly true that
only he who has struggled in secret with the mysteries of counterpoint—with the meaning of subject, counter-subject, episode, stretto—and with
the manifold complications and possibilities which
may characterize even a strict and simple fugue,
can fully appreciate the intellectual masterpieces
of Bach. The feeling that underlies their intellectual significance can no more be comprehended by
the tyro in music than a symphony conducted by
Anton Seidl can be fully appreciated by a country
maid who only plays the " Seraphine " on Sunday
afternoon. Hence the composite expression of
the audience during the Bach fugue. It might
be described as puzzled anxiety lightened by a
gleam of relief as the fugue came to an end. A
bass solo followed—Schubert's " Erl-King," sung
by a German whose magnificent delivery and neat
phrasing brought out appreciative applause. With
a placid smile he responded to an encore and
sang with unique effect a trashy English ballad.
" Goot-pye; my sheep moost zail to-night; goot-
pye, my leetle luff, goot-pye! " he shouted to the
surprised audience.

" Great Cæsar! " whispered Philip to his
sister, " why didn't you look out for his encore ? "

" Why ? because I supposed, of course, he would sing some German lied. But his sublime unconsciousness is worth seeing," she answered.

" Well, one person is pleased," continued Philip ; "look at Klinder ; he is applauding for all his soul is worth. That is the English he understands."

A 'cello solo by Klinder came next, well played with good tone and fair technique. The next number was the Raff suite. Flora seated herself at the piano ; Signor Ferranti arranged the music on the violin-stand ; the audience was absorbed in studying his appearance. Instead of the conventional evening dress, he wore a well - fitting but rusty Prince Albert coat, and trousers much looser than the prevailing fashion. His sallow face was impassive. Lifting his violin to his chin with a caressing motion, he tossed back with a quick movement of the head a lock of wavy black hair that had fallen over his forehead. A feeling of disappointment ran through the audience. They did not see the gleam of fire under his half-closed eyelids. " How old !" " How ugly !" " How stiff !" " How uninteresting !" were the comments passed from one to another. He nodded to Flora to begin.

" I am so sorry," she said ; " the music of the piano part has disappeared. I left it on the piano this afternoon." After an ineffectual search by

Philip and her father, Flora gave an appealing
glance to Signor Ferranti. "What shall we do?
what can replace it?" she asked. Signor Ferranti's eyes traveled over her as if unconsciously absorbing the effect of the stately little head crowned
with golden hair and the sweet anxious face rising above the black tulle dress. Flora's nervous
white hands rolled and unrolled the ribbon attached to a black feather fan that hung at her
waist.

"We need not change the arrangement of the
programme," he said; "we can play the Rubinstein sonata." There was a command in his eyes.
As he saw approaching dissent in her face, a mocking smile hovered about his lips. "Why are you
afraid?" he asked, harshly. Then more gently
he continued: "I am not a demon calling spirits
from the misty deep to haunt an imaginative
woman. Will you not play it with me—you, the
goddess of flowers, the embodiment of spring,
youth, and hope and love—will you play it with
me whose life is a long chill November day?"
Thrilled by the tenderness of his low, rich tones,
Flora gave assent. He placed the music before
her; his nostrils dilated, his whole figure became
animated with conscious power.

They finished the first movement. "Is this
the man whom we saw at first?" said one in the
audience to another. "He is young, he is hand-

some," whispered the young girls. Swayed by the magnetism that seemed to radiate from beneath his drooping lids, all became silent, conscious only of the wild sweetness, the fire, the longing that were poured out in mysterious waves of sound from the violin crying out like a thing of life the secrets of that world of feeling that lies beyond the reach of words. What dainty freshness of love and sunshine danced through the scherzo! Smiles curved the lips of listeners. The young dreamed of the rosy future and the old saw again the rosy past. A moment the musicians paused before striking into that strain of inspiration where like a bounding torrent the musical thought bursts all restraining barriers and carries the listener along on a flowing tide of harmony. But the hand of the violinist seems weighted, the perspiration stands on his forehead, he looks with terror toward the piano. A false chord causes him to start. With an effort he recovers himself, and the music rushes on again with brilliant freedom. A second time the strain appears. The violinist's hand trembles. The notes sound harsh and grating—produced by a powerful will struggling against some unseen influence. Nearer and nearer the players come to the sorrowing climax of the motive. Ever they struggle, hurry, then drag, as held back by mysterious power. Suddenly:

The violin gave a shriek of despair. Flora sprang up, violently dashed her hands against the empty air and grasped the arm of the violinist with a gesture of repulsion.

"I can not bear it," she cried. "Send her away! That fearful woman! What do you mean?" Her voice was shrill and sharp. For a moment they stood in this position. The violinist's hand still held the suspended bow. A gray pallor overspread his face. Flora tottered and sunk

fainting at his feet. Like a stone statue he looked
down, making no movement to lift her. Kalinski
sprang forward, muttering through his teeth :
" You shall answer to me ; you have bewitched
her with your devilish magnetism." Ferranti appeared not to hear him. Flora's father and brother
carried her out of the room. Then Ferranti
picked up the feather fan that had dropped from
her waist, laid his violin in its case, put it on the
piano, and, after fanning himself for a moment
with the long black feathers of the fan, walked
slowly and easily out of the room.

At this moment, roused as they had been to
unusual excitement by the internal fire of the music, this incident seemed perfectly natural to the
greater portion of the audience. It was a proper
climax to a period of emotional intensity. Death,
murder, suicide, would hardly have surprised the
more excitable; and it was almost with a feeling
of being cheated into commonplace acceptance of
every-day life that these latter listened to the announcement soon made by Mr. McChesney that
his daughter was merely suffering from a slight
nervous attack, and that the programme would be
continued after a brief intermission.

Nothing could have more certainly proved the
power of Signor Ferranti over an audience than
the manner in which he held attention after this
interruption. Hungarian dances wherein the

4

notes leaped from the violin like sparks of fire
preluding an outburst of sudden flame, then a
humorous scherzo through which seemed to laugh
a crowd of jostling, bustling gnomes peering above
the ground and from behind their rocky homes to
mock at the emotions of humanity, gradually
threw the listeners into a mood of sympathetic
good-humor. From the changed atmosphere it
seemed as if all had surrendered their wills to the
will of this remarkable man who remained as in-
attentive to applause as he had been to curiosity.
The pretty soprano who followed Ferranti was, in
comparison, but an animated bit of Dresden china,
piping without feeling the loves and hates of a
pygmy world. Largeness, warmth, and color came
again with the violinist; and when he carried the
players in a whirlwind of excitement through the
Beethoven quartet, a storm of applause burst forth
spontaneously and broke up all reserve as quickly
as a whirlwind breaks the brittle branches of a
forest of dead trees.

CHAPTER V.

WITHIN a week the incident that had marred the musicale had been forgotten by the guests, or, if spoken of at all, it was attributed to nervous excitement and laid away in the memory of thoughtful parents as a warning against too intimate acquaintance with professionals and too absorbing interest in one pursuit. Gossip however continued to busy itself with Signor Ferranti. With that unanimity of opinion found in some suburban towns where the inhabitants regard all foreigners with suspicion, it was confidently asserted that he was a Polish Jew of low birth, exiled to this country for political misdemeanors; that he was a Russian count, incognito, and by necessary sequence a Nihilist and a polygamist; that he was a Hindoo priest striving secretly to gain disciples in occult mysteries; that he was a Jesuit using his musical talent to lead Flora McChesney and her fortune toward the yawning portals of the Romish Church. A few business men, with no love for the divine art, pooh-poohed these surmises and declared that he was, in all probability, some poor devil from the London slums, who had found an easy way of making money through his violin and magnetic eyes, and the credulity of the gentler sex. Some of the bravest leaders of society sent him invitations to dinners and receptions; for though (they said among themselves) his name *might* be assumed his musical talent could not be, and an artist really deserved recognition; and they supplemented this noble sentiment by the private after-thought that an artist was a useful piece of odd mental bric-à-brac to stand among the ordinary collection in one's drawing-room at an afternoon tea or evening reception.

But Signor Ferranti declined all invitations. Neither for love nor money would he play excepting at the concerts in New York for which he was engaged. Neither for love nor money would he appear in any drawing-room. He remained for the most part in his room at the boarding-house; but every day he took long walks and explored the level country for miles around. During these walks he would often stand still for fifteen or twenty minutes at a time, to gaze from some elevation at the far-off horizon line where the distant water of the bay touched the bending sky; or to look, as if transfixed, at a clump of those half-developed but richly colored trees that cluster on the meadows and in the waste places near and around Medalhurst. He suffered in the estima-

tion of the inhabitants for such peculiarities. The
average resident saw no beauty in the broad open
fields, shorn of their harvest and covered now with
low stubble, dry grass, or rows of cornstalks between which might be seen the silvery whiteness
of that weed which, like a wreath of mist from sur-
rounding hills, clings to the bare ugliness of our
autumn fields; nor in the long stretches of mead-
ow shaded through all the tints of brown, gray,
and green, and lit here and there with patches of
bright red; nor in the level roads of reddish clay,
running, as if to escape from the sun, through
groves of yellow elms, red and purplish maples,
and cool green hemlocks, pines, and spruces. No;
the average resident was not discriminating in the
matter of fine shades, delicate outlines, and softly
blended harmony of sky and open field. He required a slap-dash torrent, a bold and vigorous
precipice, a mountain scaling the sky, and a cañ-
on piercing the bowels of the earth, to awaken
his stagnant love of nature. He therefore saw in
these lonely musings of Signor Ferranti only evi-
dences of cerebral inactivity which rendered the
signor indifferent alike to comment and to the
average resident of Medalhurst.

The signor was not, however, entirely indifferent to his human brethren. Once a week he dined
at the McChesneys' and remained to play in the
evening. Here in this atmosphere of courtesy, re-

finement, and appreciation, he gradually lost something of his austerity. Indeed, it may generally be noted that when genius is appreciated for its own worth, the response of genius is satisfactory. The McChesney family reaped the full reward of their comprehension. Sometimes, when music had lifted him to a mood of unwonted cheerfulness, he would delight those gathered in the music room with anecdotes of famous musicians whom he had known; he would describe their peculiarities, their different interpretations of celebrated compositions, their feats of skill; and he revealed unconsciously in these monologues that he had been on terms of intimate friendship with those of whom he spoke. Sometimes he would give his own theories in regard to the progress and development of music; and in doing so he showed that he held to the tenets of the advanced Wagnerites with all the force of a naturally warm and impetuous nature—a nature which, however controlled and repressed by the deep sorrows which had evidently chilled his intercourse with humanity in general, would betray itself in these earnest talks. But he also showed to his listeners that in the liberality and soundness of his views he far surpassed the partisan followers of Wagner.

"I believe," he said one evening in answer to a question from Mr. McChesney, "that in Wagner's music we have the legitimate climax of all

that has gone before in musical expression; and
that we all have the right to push on beyond
Wagner if we choose—or perhaps I should say, if
we can—only limiting ourselves or being limited
by our superiors in the knowledge of the general
laws of art, and by our own capacity of interpretation. If any one, like Spontini or Berlioz, feels
within himself a power of forceful dramatic expression which enables him to draw out orches-
trally the hidden meaning of a subject or a phrase
and to impress it strongly upon a listener's mind,
such a one must be true to his own insight, however he may be laughed at by contemporaries.
Otherwise, he is unworthy the name of musician."

"Certainly," said Mr. McChesney, taking advantage of Ferranti's momentary hesitation, "certainly. The searcher after truth must learn to
pay no attention to the bickerings in Philistia.
If he does, he will end literally by flinging his
earnestness to the dogs."

"Impoverishing himself to furnish them with
a temporary bone of contention," added Philip,
expansively.

"The true musician, the true composer," continued Ferranti, with that steady, unseeing gaze
which betokens a man too occupied with the main
current of thought to heed its murmuring tribu-
taries, "the true genius shall seek constantly for
new effects, for new combinations of old laws; the

performer shall recognize that the power of reproducing is in reality of the same value as the power of creation, for without reproduction creative work can not live; and the performer or interpreter shall not hesitate to increase effects beyond the limit set by the composer, if the spirit of the times compels. He must consider particularly the composer's relation to the time when his work is presented, which time may require a different degree of intensity in emotional expression from that required by the time when his work was created. The performer or interpreter must, of course, from this point of view, have the delicate perception of a true artist, and an accurate knowledge of the requirements of his own age. The listener and the critic, too (who should, in order to criticise this most subtle of all arts, be a born musician) ought always to hold themselves in the attitude of those who would further and not hinder progress. Educated by the genius of Wagner, there will probably be in days to come a composer who will surpass Wagner. Orchestral improvements still broader, 'regular irregularities' of form, and new rhythmic effects will be the coming composer's weapons to rule the musical world."

"You give him a hopeless task when you ask that he shall surpass Wagner," Kalinski said. "How can he?"

"First, by becoming thoroughly familiar with

all the theories upon which Wagner's masterpieces
are built. While Wagner is a poor guide as a
musical critic, since he was unable to focus his
gaze correctly upon his contemporaries, he is the
most remarkable teacher of musical ethics that
has yet appeared. Wagner did not write his
works according to his theories, but wrote his
theories according to his works. His works show
the spontaneity of genius; and the philosophical
laws that he gives us are the aftermath of a genius.
From the philosophical nature of his mind, from
his instinctive grasping for eternal laws, his operas
reveal, as Beethoven's symphonies reveal, an ever-
ascending scale of completeness. Now, the coming musician must absorb all that has been done,
must place himself in sympathy with his own age,
and yet perceive, with the intuition of genius,
the wants of the age to come, as Wagner understood his own and the coming age. The restless spirit of modern life has found expression
through Wagner's genius in modern music; as the
restlessness of a previous time found grand and
satisfactory solution in the sublimity and peace of
Beethoven's greatest works, so ought the restless
intellectual excitement that animates the works
of Berlioz, Rubinstein, Dvorák, Brahms, and Wagner find at length its triumphant resolution in
some master of a coming age who, with all the
resources these workers have gathered, will use

them to show once more to humanity, in the divinest of all arts, the peace that comes in cycles to the great world-soul struggling upward step by step. The triumph shall come again as in Beethoven—submission to the will of the universe, obedience to ultimate good."

"And out of what land shall come thiss—Weltbezwinger?" asked Klinder, gazing placidly over his spectacles at the enthusiastic speaker.

Kalinski sprang up quickly. "France! The whole progress of music shows the power of France. Italy was ruled by her, Germany had to learn from her in order to gain present supremacy. France has dramatic intensity, quick perception, and the intellect to seize an opportunity."

Klinder looked with inexpressible scorn at the Russo-Frenchman. "S-s-o? Ye-e-s," he said, slowly; "France can always seize the right opportunity—at the wrong time."

"America," said Mr. McChesney, "is really most likely to be the birthplace of this genius, perhaps even in another century. The American shows in art the resistless spirit of progress; he scorns tradition, he seeks new laws, and by the fusion of various nationalities he will acquire German thoroughness, French vivacity, Italian warmth, and Russian force."

"Japanese patience, Scotch shrewdness, and Irish humor you should add to your list of ingredi-

ents for making a genius. With due deference to
you, father, I say that genius can't very well be
molded in the pudding-dish of any one's imagination. A genius, to my mind, is a sort of miracle
created at any time and at any place by the operation of unknown laws." Philip said this earnestly,
and then, as if his dictum settled the matter, he
walked to the piano and began to wrestle with the
intricate chords of the Pilgrim's chorus from
" Tannhäuser."

Kalinski was the only one who never took
such conversations with good-humor. His inward
rebellion at Ferranti's influence and superior mental powers manifested itself on this evening, as on
several others, by asserting the dignity of the
second violin above the first. They played this
night some of Haydn's string quartets, which,
however unsatisfactory in harmonic treatment to
ears trained to the richer modulations of Schumann, Beethoven, and Wagner, yet impress any
genuine musician with their varying and melodi-
ous themes and exquisite unity of form. In a
broad and simple adagio Kalinski's petty spiteful-
ness hatefully obtruded through the calm and tender sentiment of the movement. Ferranti took
no notice of any eccentricities until the end of the
adagio. Then, laying down his violin, he pointed
to the bust of Haydn looking down majestically
from the gallery.

"How do you think that manner of playing would suit the composer? A true musician forgets himself and his own secret annoyances when he tries to interpret the great masters. You do yourself injustice."

At this gentle but just rebuke, Kalinski reddened, bit his lip, and showed for an instant the gleam of white teeth under his bristling black mustache.

When Kalinski went away Philip went with him to the hall. As Kalinski drew on his overcoat abruptly, he gazed at Philip with a wild stare of unhappiness. "I am going mad, I believe. Oh! if *he* had never come your sister might have loved me! Already she had begun to trust me. And I must see him take her from me! Mon Dieu! Ma peine—que c'est affreuse!" and he brushed his hand swiftly across his forehead.

"Ah, my dear old friend," said Philip, placing his hand gently upon Kalinski's shoulder, "believe me, your theories are wrong. If my sister could have loved you or had loved you, no other man could win her from you. She is not a weak-minded girl to be swayed by changing fancies. And you are mistaken. Ferranti seldom speaks to her; he talks to father and myself; he has a heart only for his violin. Her interest and sympathy are those of one musician for another. These feelings are unworthy of you."

In Philip's honest brown eyes gleamed so divine a tenderness that the bitterness passed out of Kalinski's face as suddenly as a shadow is banished by a sunbeam. He grasped Philip's hand silently, and silently went out into the night.

CHAPTER VI.

WHILE it was quite true, as Philip said, that Ferranti had apparently made no attempt to win Flora's favor and had apparently bestowed his attention entirely upon Mr. McChesney and Philip, there was yet an undercurrent of feeling between the signor and Flora that ran too deep for even an interested observer to perceive. Although Flora McChesney was too proud to give her love unsought, she was strongly attracted by the first man of intellect and refinement who had so long remained indifferent to her charms. A true woman in this respect she indulged in much speculation as to the causes of his silence and indifference. Only in the music could she feel that his spirit spoke to hers. Now and then she caught a glance of admiration at the end of some brilliant passage of great difficulty, or heard a word of praise in Italian, spoken as if to himself, when she had followed his mood with perfect comprehension in some concerted piece. So it had been until one afternoon soon after the preceding brief conversation between Philip and Kalinski. Ferranti had come to play a new sonata for piano and violin by Heinrich Hoffmann. They were alone in the music room, and both played with that enthusiasm which inspires the musician at the first trial of a new and interesting composition. Flora surpassed herself, conquering technical difficulties with unusual ease and accuracy.

"I could never do that again," she sighed, as she closed the music and looked up at him, her cheeks red with excitement. "It is your magnificent playing that lifts me above myself."

Ferranti came and stood close beside her, and bent upon her a look of such earnestness that, disturbed by the feeling in his eyes, she dropped her own while the color crept to her very forehead. He put out his hand and clasped hers with a warm, strong grasp. There was no need of words; Flora knew in that moment that they loved each other— that their souls had met in spiritual union—divine prelude to the blending of two earthly songs in one harmonious strain. But Ferranti dropped her hand almost as quickly as he had taken it. He turned away and walked to the window, where he stood, neither of them could have told how long, watching the snow fast falling over the pine trees and the bare elm branches, and covering with its quiet flakes the level stretch of lawn that sloped downward from the house. Presently he came toward her again; but all life and animation had

vanished from his face. He seemed not to have
sufficient vitality even to toss back the lock of
hair which had fallen over his forehead and
which intensified by its blackness the gray pall-
or of the face. Forgetting herself and all other
feeling save that of tender sympathy, Flora said
gently:

"Oh, signor, can not you be happy in your
music?"

By these words she recognized the affection he
had not told, and also the barrier that existed to
separate them. Ferranti understood her.

"Signorina," he said in a low tone as he drew
a chair near the piano. "The snow is falling fast
outside, the trees are bare, the earth is still and
lifeless; but it is only for a time; the spring will
bring fresh blossoms from the earth, young golden-
green leaves from the withered trees, and rays of
tender sunlight will shine upon the lawn in place
of the cold white snow. Not so with my life;
there it must be winter now and forever. Only
in my music do I find sunshine. But I ought not
to sadden your life even for a moment with sorrows of my own. Once—"

He bit his lip and checked the coming words.

"But the world is before you to conquer with
your music. Nature and art are both ready to
soothe your troubles and to give you peace, even if
you can not have the highest happiness. And is

it nothing that friends are near you to give you silent sympathy?"

Ferranti gave an expressive backward movement of the hand.

"Fame? Only to him who can not win it does it gleam like a star instead of a bit of colored glass. Nature breathes of love; art, too, whispers of love, of warm human affection which may not, must not, be mine."

A chill struck to Flora's heart. But though she felt the determination and the despair of these words, she could not be altogether unhappy. He loved her, he would have told her so if he could. Love came to her, as to so many others, hand in hand with sorrow; but at least she was not cheated of her right to know his love. This for the moment was supreme consolation and lightened the shadow of necessary repression. She did not attempt during the silence that ensued to evade the questions that came before her; she did not disguise to herself, as a weaker woman might, the fact that she loved the man of whom she knew so little and who could not tell her of his love; she accepted the inevitable, the bitter with the sweet, and she knew instinctively, even though she could not formulate her knowledge, that these holy flames now flashing across her heart would prove a purifying fire and not an all-consuming fire.

Presently he went on in a low, gentle tone:

5

"There was once a man walking through a forest. His way had been rough and full of dangers, his journey long and tiresome. He was lonely and unhappy. Just as he was thinking bitter thoughts he stepped into an open place where the blue sky arched above the delicate lacings of the tree tops, and the warm sun touched with gold the lusty banks of ferns that seemed to bound in joyous life away into the shadows of the pine trees guarding the rocky hills on either side. A white dove fluttered down from an overhanging branch, lit on his hand and pecked at his sleeve; to him it was the expression of sympathy from all-powerful Nature. As he held for a moment the tender fluttering thing in his strong hands, the thought crossed his mind to endeavor to imprison it, to woo it to always cheer his solitude, to be the tangible link between him and the warm human world. But better thoughts prevailed. What! cage it from the sunny freedom of an unstained life? For a selfish pleasure of his own to hold it in bondage? No! a thousand times, no!"

And Ferranti here arose and grasped the chair-back firmly with one hand while he raised the other with a fervid gesture. He lowered his voice again as he dropped his hand.

"Tenderness and protection for the loveliest of God's creatures who know not their own danger is the duty of the strong. The man, tired and

hungry and desolate as he might be, saw no excuse
for caging the dove that innocently fluttered near
him. He held his hands; and he watched the
dove soar again to the freedom of the upper blue
and fade, far in the distance, into the pure white
clouds beyond his reach."

The rich, musical tones died away in almost a
whisper. Flora had looked steadily in his face as
he spoke, and, won by the spiritual gentleness
which softened the lines of suffering, she went up
to him with instinctive confidence and laid her
hand upon the slender nervous hand that rested
still on the back of the chair.

" You will be my friend ? " she said quietly.

" Always; God grant it, signorina," he said, in
a repressed, husky voice; but he made no movement to detain her as she left the room.

After this day Flora allowed herself no intercourse with Ferranti save through the music which
they played together. Although he seemed a
shade more melancholy, and seemed daily to grow
thinner, he talked more brilliantly than ever, rous-
ing always the best thoughts of others and giving
out unstintedly the treasures of knowledge he had
accumulated. He had known how to throw away
the chaff and put rich golden grain into the great
storehouse of memory, and he was not one of
those intellectual misers who, fearing to benefit
some poorer brother whom circumstance would

not permit to glean the field of wisdom, leave the harvest they have gathered to rot in musty richness. He recognized that the law of life is to give freely; so only shall one be saved from the torpor—death.

CHAPTER VII.

THE winter passed quietly away. Mr. Mc-Chesney interested himself more and more in the collection of rare manuscripts, a hobby to which a new impetus had been given by the gift from Ferranti of original scores of Beethoven, Mozart, and Mendelssohn. Kalinski kept persistently away from the house, so Philip with some instruction from Ferranti had developed his natural talent so far as to be able to fill Kalinski's place in the quartet. Had it not been for a certain languor and occasional fits of depression which Mrs. McChesney noticed in Flora and which aroused some uneasiness in her mother's mind, there would have been nothing to mar the even tenor of life at Strathcarron.

One evening in early March they were all gathered in the music room. It was one of those evenings when the frosty air and blustering winds without cause one to turn with keen appreciation to the cheerfulness within. They were all especially merry, and when the door-bell rang and the voice of Kalinski was heard, Flora made a charming little moue at Ferranti and elevated her

eyebrows as if to say "Now our comfort will be
spoiled." Kalinski entered, inflated with good-
humor, like some previously despondent rubber
cushion with its long-forgotten quota of air. He
seemed much taller than usual. His bushy whiskers were parted and carefully brushed each way,
while his bristling hair being closely cropped no
longer intensified his aggressive facial character-
istics. He was faultlessly dressed, wore a red carnation in his button-hole, and, contrary to his usual
custom, had seen that his nails were carefully pol-
ished and trimmed. He proceeded to make himself universally agreeable, even to the extent of
politeness to Signor Ferranti. He took his usual
place in the quartet.

"What is going to happen?" said Flora, as she
crossed the room and sat down on a low divan
near the large easy-chair occupied by her mother.
"Mr. Kalinski is himself again. He is almost en-
durable to-night. He seems possessed by some
pleasant secret. Perhaps he has fallen in love
with some responsive being."

"Ah, my dear, that is the first thing you young
people think of as desirable. Let us think of him
as having met with some material piece of good
fortune."

"Why, mother, how can you! You—to be
cynical, when you have been so happy yourself!
Is there any greater blessing than—"

"My child," said the mother, with a soft sigh, "I was not thinking of myself." And her eyes dwelt a moment on her daughter's rounded cheek and then wandered on to the sallow profile of the Italian who was bending over some music at the other end of the room. Ah, that mother instinct! too keen to be thwarted even by the seemingly placid exterior of a loved child! Guided only by instinct, the mother goes to the hoarded store of sweetness within the shrinking heart as unerringly as the wild bee speeds his way to the honey in far-off apple blooms. She will read the signs of secret trouble that no other eye can see, and grasp your every thought while you fondly think your sorrows are your own. But if she be a wise mother she bides her time for speaking. Though not a woman of great mental power, Mrs. McChesney possessed the rare virtue of knowing when to talk and when to keep silent. For the present, then, she leaned back easily in her chair with her fleecy white-wool knitting in her hands; but she now and then cast a thoughtful glance at Flora's graceful Psyche-like head, bent slightly forward in rapt attention to the exquisite harmonies that proceeded from the now sympathetic quartet.

"This Schubert music, coming after the Brahms movement, is like the music of a running brook coming after the clatter of a saw mill," said Philip when the last chords died away.

"Or rather," said Flora quickly, "like a smiling landscape after a thunder-storm; for Brahms is strong and powerful, and he has a definite place in music, as the thunder and lightning have in the world of nature. He seems rough indeed sometimes, when he breaks over the forms and conventionalities of a past age, but he opens the way for new beauties in the music landscape. Destruction must prepare the way for improvement. Brahms is more a destroyer than a beautifier; but his music is never like the clatter of a saw mill. I am surprised at you, Philip!" and Flora tried to frown.

"Don't be hard on a clumsy fellow, Flo. That was only a figure of speech."

"A decidedly wooden one, too," answered Flora; "like the Indian before a cigar store."

"Pointing to treasures within?"

"Yes; which end in smoke."

"You seem to like the indicative mood, belle sœur," Philip quickly continued.

"*And* present tense."

"Or tense present," laughed Philip. "Women seldom generalize enough to use future tenses."

"But they particularize well," answered Flora; "and it is from details that men are enabled to generalize."

"Oh, surely; I grant that to particular eyes

men owe much knowledge of a certain kind.
Doesn't Moore say—

> My only books were women's looks,
> And folly's all they've taught me."

"But what does the greater Shakespeare say?
spoke Ferranti quickly, noting in a flash Flora's
nonplused look.

> "From women's eyes this doctrine I derive:
> They sparkle still the right Promethean fire;
> They are the books, the arts, the Academes—
> That show contain and nourish all the world."

"Two against one—no wonder I am beaten,"
Philip exclaimed.

"But apropos of Brahms," said Ferranti, returning Flora's grateful glance with a half smile;
"Do you remember the story told not long ago
about Von Bülow conducting a Brahms symphony
at Vienna?"

"No," said Philip; "let's have it. A plaster,
I suppose, to soothe my lacerated logic."

"That is as you take it," answered Ferranti.
"But here it is, shorter than the prelude. Well,
it was a new composition, and evidently exercised a depressing effect upon musicians as well
as upon dilettanti and tyros who were present.
At the close of the symphony there was profound
silence. Von Bülow, waiting for the applause that
did not come, calmly surveyed the audience. 'Ev-

idently the audience does not understand the symphony,' he said in a loud tone. 'We will play it over again.' And the orchestra played it over again. After which there was no lack of applause."

"That is very like him, according to all accounts," said Mr. McChesney.

"He has to father a good many eccentricities that he has no kinship with," Ferranti said. "He happens to be a convenient peg on which to hang the odds and ends of musical gossip. He is in reality one of the most delightful, well-bred, and generous men in the world; but he has a high conception of his own dignity and the dignity of his profession."

"Do you believe" Kalinski asked, suddenly rising and assuming a somewhat theatrical attitude which seemed the studied climax of some train of thought, "that one could tell a story by a musical instrument so clearly that a musical listener could understand the story without the addition of words?"

Ferranti was leaning against the piano, his arms folded and his head bent slightly forward. A quizzical gleam crossed his face at the question.

"No, indeed." He spoke in an indulgent tone. "I only believe that the general atmosphere of a composition is comprehended by a musical mind. There is a difference between imaginative and romantic music, you know. Imaginative music of the highest grade appeals to the musical mind in a language incomprehensible to the ordinary listener; it deals with abstract musical thoughts. Romantic music represents some scene or event that has place in the composer's mind and around which he groups his musical expressions. The andante from the fifth symphony, the scherzo from the seventh are good examples of the former, while the pastoral symphony is one of the most familiar and satisfactory examples of the latter. An ordinary passionate composition of the romantic school certainly requires a clew to be given to its meaning. The music to one listener may represent a real storm, to another, a quarrel between two lovers or a tragedy in which revenge has proved the key-note. Calm moonlight on the sea, or a happy maiden reverie in the summer wood, or the quiet of accepted love, may all be given in the same musical expressions. The listener's mind colors the musical impressions which it receives. The significance, I insist, of musical phrases is comprehended only by musical feeling; they can not be presented satisfactorily to another's mind by material images, although it be desirable for the composer to so present them in order to point to the ordinary listener the direction in which his thoughts are to be turned. Even with direction the thoughts of the listener are very apt to cluster around material images very different from those that sprang up in the composer's mind as he wrote. The listener's images are in harmony with the general tenor of his thoughts and the general habits of his life."

"Then, of course, you do not believe that there is any such thing as music, sensuous per se?" interpolated Mr. McChesney.

"Of course not. A soft, grave hymn, or a light scherzo expressive of pure and happy childlife, may become, if used in vulgar surroundings, a medium to a vulgar mind of impure thoughts; but the music itself remains pure, and can not be degraded by a beer-saloon or a Jardin Mabille."

"Now," said Kalinski, "I have a story to tell upon the violin. As you think it could not be understood without explanation, I will accompany the music with appropriate words. This will afford you all a novel and instructive entertainment."

Philip laughed under his breath and glanced at Ferranti. "Aha," said he aloud, "a musical drama in—how many acts? Something, perhaps, on the principle of the early art forms which preceded the oratorio and the opera—a sort of cantata with a slight accompaniment—an aria recitativo with a figured bass on the violin."

Kalinski looked at him unseeingly, and began at once his peculiar performance. He had some facility of description, and the words tripped smoothly from his tongue as soon as he began his story.

Before each scene he gave a musical overture which included the principal events and emotions, and, in addition, whenever a character appeared for the first time he would give a characteristic musical portrait of the mental qualities. His evident intent to be taken seriously compelled his auditors to stifle all tendency to amusement, and to listen with some degree of courtesy. Moreover, they were all musicians in spirit if not in fact, and Kalinski, always more or less dramatic, now showed in his playing fire and force which commended him to their favor.

CHAPTER VIII.

It is a festa day in the month of May at Rome. The odorous acacia blossoms, the golden gorse, the wild sweet-pea, and a host of dainty creeping vines and flowering weeds clamber along the hedges outside the city, and millions of scarlet poppies blaze amid the swaying grain upon the broad Campagna. The goat-herd comes down from the mountain; the peasant, the monk, the soldier jostle each other on the crowded streets; the women sing and laugh from their open windows, or chatter in musical voices under the gray-stone walls crowned with red blossoms of the spicy oleander. As the warm sun sinks slowly westward in a sea of fire, the sounds of guitars and violins fall upon the ear, the scent of orange blossoms fills the air, and welcome to the taste is the sherbet or lemonade from the canvas-covered booths on every plaza. Shrines are erected at the corners of the streets; and beneath one of these crude pictures of the Madonna before which burns constantly a little light, kneels a young peas-

ant girl saying her rosary with pious care. A young
Italian, well-dressed, handsome, and evidently of
noble birth, watches her attentively. At Ave
Maria, when dove-like twilight broods over the
city and the open fields, a great procession takes
place—the chanting priests circle through the
plaza, church-banners float above their heads,
the crowd bends before the ostia. When it disappears, and the people gather before the church to
look at the tapestried platform and to listen to
the music of the band, the young cavalier may
be seen talking and jesting with the peasant girl.
Dressed now himself as a peasant, he wears white
stockings, a tall hat with rosettes, and a loose black
velvet jacket. The girl is dressed like others of
her class and province, in a light bodice and a
silken skirt, and above her white chemise a coral
necklace rests upon her full brown neck and bosom.
From her ears hang heavy ear-rings of gold, and
her thick black braids are looped up neatly around
her handsome head. They are very gay, these
young people; and the bells ring and the organ
peals, and flowers and crucifixes and banners are
everywhere along the streets. Why should they
not be gay? It is May, and May is the time for
love. By and by the young signor and Anita (for
that is her name) slip away from the old peasant
woman with whom Anita has come down from the
mountains, and join a merry group on the edge of

the crowd where sounds the sharp click of the casta-
nets and the dull thrum of the tambourines. Who
can dance the saltarello like this rosy-cheeked,
luminous-eyed Anita, flashing her dark eyes be-
witchingly and throwing her lithe, elastic form
into a thousand graceful, changing curves, unless
it be the young signor, circling around her with
quick, short steps, clapping his hands, and begging
for the kiss which she will refuse again and again
only to yield in pantomime at last. If it were
only always in pantomime!

. . . . . .

Now they are among the green forests that
wind around the Alban Lake. They are on the
way to that summit where once stood the temple
of Jupiter Latialis, and where now stands the con-
vent of Monte Cavi. From here they will look
down on the Roman Campagna, its fields of plumy
grasses and parti-colored flowers waving in rhythmic motion to the wind-harps of the golden-
trunked pines; its ilex trees and luxuriant vines
covering the jagged angles of broken bridges,
tombs, and aqueducts; and its brown banks re-
minding you of the catacombs that underlie this
brilliant stretch of color—more brilliant under
the purple and gold of sunset that rests along the
far horizon line. But Anita and her cavalier
think not of the light and nature-life around
them, nor of the generations of dead that lie be-

neath them. They see only the love-light in each
other's eyes. Presently, when the moon shines
full and clear in the heavens, they are at a rustic
dance in an old castle. Nightingales sing in the
ilex groves, and laurels shadow the narrow paths
where they can wander when heated with the
dance. Nobles and peasants dance freely together
on the brick floor of the great half-ruined hall.
Of all the contadini who is so charming as Anita,
the Albanian maiden! And who so worthy of her
glances as the peasant noble who whispers in her ear
the sweet nothings that spring from a lover's heart!

.   .   .   .   .   .

One evening, at a villetta on the mountain-side,
an old woman wrings her hands as she sits alone
among the vines and vegetables of her little garden. Under the arbor, upon which the warm
autumn sun has shone all day with quiet force,
she sits and moans, while the tears run down her
withered cheeks. The vintage festival has come
and gone. Gone are the laughing peasants, strong
of back and sturdy of limb, their heads and faces
stained with the purple grape ; gone are the bas-
ket-wagons and the oxen decked with vines and
bright-hued ribbons; gone is the handsome Bac-
chus who, crowned with ivy and bearing a sheep-
skin over his shoulder, headed the vintage procession ; gone, too, is the fairest of the maidens who
followed, with a basket of grapes upon her stately

6

head and a vine-wreath around her neck brown-
tinted by the mellowing sun. Gone are they all.
Everything is still. Even the goats browse no
longer on the juicy herbs covering the fertile
hills. Only the full moon looks quietly down
upon the gray-green olives nestling upon the um-
ber-hued hills, and touches with an added gleam
of silver the gray hair of the lonely mother wring-
ing her hands in grief. On the seat beside her
lies a letter which was read to her at sunset by
the parish priest. At one moment she snatches
it up and kisses it with a pitiful cry, and the next,
she flings it from her with a gesture of contempt.
She can not follow Anita; she is poor; since her
husband's death she has toiled daily with her
hands to keep a home for the bright-eyed, laughing girl who is now so far away. She bows her
head in despair as she feels the numbness of coming desolation creep slowly through her heart.
She grows more quiet while the night hours wear
away; she does not feel the chill night dews that
fall upon her, nor the chill night wind that tosses
her gray hair. The morning sun at last peers under the grape-hung trellis, but he is powerless to
warm the cold body stretched out upon the narrow
seat, the withered face upturned as if imploring
pity from the bending sky. The mother-heart
has broken; the toil-worn body is at rest.

.   .   .   .   .   .

On the corner of a semi-respectable street in
Paris stands one of those damp and dingy structures in which decayed gentility finds a squalid
refuge. Here, in an ill-ventilated, cheaply fur-
nished room, is immured the charming peasant
taken from the free air of the Roman hills. A
year goes by on swift and rosy wings. Another
year; but its wings are leaden, and it flings a
shadow over the brightness of Anita's face. He
neglects her now, this lover who could not live
without her. Long hours she is left alone, to
watch the tall, straight walls that front the small-
paned windows, or to count the shepherds and
shepherdesses on the figured paper of her room—
happy youths and maidens who recall her own
lost happiness and intensify by their unending
joy the fleeting nature of her own. She has no
power to amuse herself in this frothy world of
gayety revolving about her in the distance.
She has a tender, loving heart, poor weak Anita.
Evening after evening she weeps her bitter tears
and eats the ashes of her hopes; evening after
evening she sees him for a moment in his well-
fitting evening dress and dainty gloves, and then
she watches him roll away in a well-appointed
dark-green cabriolet to the salons where she
may never go. The coachman smacks his whip;
the young Italian nods; houp la! what matters a
heavy heart or two when Pleasure's finger beck-

ons? The world wags right merrily for those who know how to take it. One day there is a violent scene. Hot words pass. Anita learns too late that she is as free to go as she was free to follow— nay, a thousand times more free, for she followed by the constraining power of love. She learns too late that to put faith in a lover's word is to put faith in a brittle sword. That night she flies. She will never return. And the young Italian goes gayly on his way, happy in his recovered freedom, serenely conscious that she has left him of her own accord. He is not rich; now he will retrieve his fortunes. And Anita? Pouf! He takes his cigarette from his mouth: pouf! a blue ring of smoke disappears.

. . . . . .

CHAPTER IX.

WHEN Kalinski had reached this point in his story he stood nearly opposite Flora and her mother. He laid his violin bow on an adjacent stand, and then, with a dramatic gesture, he drew from the inner breast-pocket of his coat two photographs. "Here," said he, "is the girl whose story I have told. In this see her beauty, her grace, her innocence; in that see her as she looks out from the barred windows of an asylum and calls in vain for the lover who does not come."

Mrs. McChesney took the photographs, holding them so that the upper picture hid the lower. Flora leaned over the arm of the chair to look at them. "What a lovely face," she exclaimed, "I never saw a more perfect oval; and those large dark eyes, so Madonna-like and mournful. Could any man destroy the happiness of such a woman? See, mother, on her neck she wears a cross attached to a small chain; and that square head-dress makes her look like one of the sisters at St. Mary's. Oh, the story is too cruel! It can not be true!"

"I hardly understand your idea, Mr. Kalinski," said Mrs. McChesney, "in telling us a story of this kind. Could you not have selected something more suitable to entertain us with?" She elevated her eybrows rather haughtily and surveyed him coldly.

"But let me see the other picture," interrupted Flora. She took it from her mother, gave it one eager glance, and dropped it as though it burned her fingers. "It is the same face; I have seen it twice before," she said, in a low, choked voice through which vibrated a tone of horror. She shuddered and covered her face with both hands.

"Bien, madame; you see my idea?" Kalinski addressed Mrs. McChesney with a triumphant smile. "And there," he continued, wheeling around so as to face Ferranti, "there is the man who loved this girl, who deserted her, who ruined her happiness."

Ferranti still stood motionless, leaning against the piano; still kept his arms tightly folded. He straightened himself now and came forward, his face pale, his head thrown back, and his arms still more tightly clasped, as if to confine the words that struggled for utterance. His throat swelled, and his eyes flashed beneath his dark and knitted brows as smoldering sparks flash beneath charred embers.

He spoke directly to Kalinski, in slow and

careful, measured tones: "Your story is highly
interesting. Permit me, though, to correct it in
one important respect. This woman whose picture you have obtained was, and is, my lawful
wife. The marriage certificate and various con-
vincing letters are in my possession, and can be
shown any moment in proof of what I say. I
have, moreover—a fact of which you have carefully
neglected to inform yourself—a son about six
years of age, who is now with my mother in Italy.
I am supporting both my mother and my son to
the best of my ability, as well as my wife, who
receives the best care and attention that can be
found for her in her unfortunate condition. My
marriage, which took place under an assumed
name, was kept secret for family reasons, and
ought still to be kept secret for some time. It
will not be long before the reasons for secrecy
will have ceased to exist, and I shall then be able
·to publicly acknowledge my son. This explanation is made," he continued scornfully, "not by
any means on *your* account, but out of respect to
the family who have received me with a courtesy
and hospitality which I can never forget." After
a moment's pause, he added: "There are a good
many minor mistakes, too, in the story which you
have maliciously constructed upon a slight founda-
tion. But to correct them involves my revealing
private sorrows and details of the private life of

others, and I do not feel justified in doing this. The cause of my unfortunate wife's insanity is evidently quite unknown to you. How you have gained this knowledge, this slight basis upon which you have reared a flimsy structure of absurdities, is quite beyond my comprehension. Perhaps you will kindly inform me; and perhaps, also, you will give me my right name, which is not yet known to the people of Medalhurst." He shot a piercing glance at Kalinski with these words, a glance which Kalinski refused to meet. Indeed, he seemed greatly taken aback at this straightforward challenge, and lost countenance immediately. His expression of triumph faded to one of doubt. After some hesitation, during which there was an embarrassing silence, Kalinski drew from the same pocket of his coat which had held the two photographs a few loose sheets of paper, dangling irregularly from a thread which caught them together.

"Ah," said Ferranti impassively, "so Mr. Emil Kalinski conspires with servants; he lights his rockets at the kitchen fire and turns the poker for divining rod."

"It is not so," Kalinski answered sharply, reddening at the same time. "The papers, I found them in the barrel—the barrel of ashes, of débris outside the house; the wind blew them, I gave them some blows of my foot, I picked them up—voilà tout!"

"I remember them—some loose leaves of an old diary. And soon after you came to spend the evening with me. On a tour of inspection? And the photographs?" Ferranti still maintained his tone of stinging courtesy; but he had fastened his compelling eyes sternly upon Kalinski.

"I—I—borrowed them," muttered the crest-fallen man, constrained to answer against his will. The ludicrous lameness of this answer could not but bring a smile to the lips of Philip and his father. So nearly do pathos and bathos touch in moments of supreme excitement. Every one remained silent for some little time. Mrs. McChesney held the first picture of the Italian girl, and contemplated it reflectively; Flora kept her face buried in her hands; Mr. McChesney and Philip evidently considered silence the better part of discretion, the former occupying himself by stroking his mustache with the spread-out thumb and fingers of his left hand, the latter twisting his legs in a bow-knot under an inoffensive chair which he was rapidly despoiling of its ornamental fringe; Karl Klinder took off his spectacles and proceeded to give them an efficient but needless polishing with his red silk handkerchief.

The tables, for a few moments at least, had been unexpectedly turned. Marvelous self-control, enabled Ferranti to stand before the little group rather in the attitude of a judge before a

group of criminals than that of a prisoner before
a jury. The nervous tension of the moment was
relieved by his stooping to pick up the photo-
graph that Flora had dropped upon the floor.
He asked for the one held by Mrs. McChesney,
placed them both together, and slipped them under
the orange silk cover that protected his violin.
This commonplace movement and the composure
with which he locked the case, turning the key
in the lock with a vigorous snap, brought them
back to a sense of every-day life. Mr. McChesney rose and made a forward movement as if to
address Ferranti. Kalinski anticipated him.

"And the face that appeared to Miss Flora?
How does Signor Ferranti explain it!"

"Be careful, sir," said Mr. McChesney, suddenly and explosively, "this matter has gone far
enough! No further comments are necessary.
Both you and Signor Ferranti are guests in my
house; do not you, sir, compel me to forget my
present duty as your host."

"Allow me to bid you good evening," said
Ferranti to Mrs. McChesney, who slightly bowed
in return. "Adieu, signorina," to Flora, who had
not taken her hands from her face. His voice
was not so firm as he uttered these two words.
Bowing then to the men in the room collectively,
he pushed aside the velvet portière, against which
his pale, aquiline features and black hair and aris-

tocratic figure stood out in high relief. At this moment Flora suddenly rose and swept across the room, her long, black dress folding closely around her and giving added dignity to her slender form, drawn now to its full height.

"Signor Ferranti," said she earnestly, offering him her hand, "I believe your explanation; I believe your actions have been those of an honorable man. You have my sympathy for your present sorrow and my earnest hopes for your success and future happiness."

Ferranti dropped the curtain, and an expression of acute anguish crossed his face. He bent forward to gravely imprint a kiss upon her extended hand.

Flora stood still as he left the room. The cold, tremulous lips and the clammy fingers that had touched her own revealed the strain through which the strong, sensitive nature had passed. She felt instinctively that a farewell had been spoken, that through this farewell had breathed resignation to those higher spiritual laws which forbid revenge or hatred or malice of a mortal toward even the meanest of God's creatures; and through this farewell had also breathed the tenderness and pride that would in future hold him far away from the woman whom he loved.

The voice of Mr. McChesney roused Flora from her sad reflections. "My daughter," said he, "are you not over-impulsive? We really do not know, excepting from SignorFerranti's own words, that he is not masquerading in borrowed plumage. We know he is an agreeable man, but it seems to me we ought to withhold our judgment for the present."

"Father, your common sense is struggling hard to gain the victory over feeling; but you know as well as I that his words and manner bear the stamp of truth."

Mr. McChesney shook his head deprecatingly, although he had been more impressed than he cared to acknowledge by Ferranti's quiet dignity.

"As for you," continued Flora scornfully, turning to Kalinski, "you have maliciously dragged to light the misfortunes of an artist and of a man whose shoe-latchets you are not worthy to unloose. You need not expect from *me* the forbearance with which you have been treated by my father and mother."

Kalinski's face grew dark, and he muttered, in a sort of currish snarl, "He is a coward, this Signor Ferranti."

"Coward, do you say?" replied Flora. "He is brave and manly enough to bear an imputation of cowardice from you, out of respect to us. And you well know his simple, straightforward statement is true in every particular."

"Flora, your defense of Signor Ferranti is very

uncalled for," said Mrs. McChesney, speaking in a
higher key than usual and gathering up her
worsted work preparatory to leaving the room.
" Whatever he may be as an artist, he is, according to his own statement, under a serious cloud,
and certainly he is married and he is obliged to
conceal the fact. I don't'like all this deception,
and I prefer that Signor Ferranti should not enter
my house again." And Mrs. McChesney adjusted
her fleecy shawl about her shoulders and shook
down the folds of her drapery, very much as a
motherly hen, foreseeing danger to her callow
brood, ruffles her feathers with an aggressive air
and gives vent to her anxiety by staccato clucks
and cackles.

" My dear, my dear," said Mr. McChesney,
with a suspicion of a smile.

" Well, you never think my judgment is worth
anything, but I tell you there may lie more danger
than you think in his future visits."

" I think you are mistaken, Josephine." Mr.
McChesney rarely called his wife by the stately
name which seemed inappropriate to her rotund
figure and amiable face; whenever he did so, it
indicated a subtle rebuke. " This is really a prof-
itless subject of discussion," he added, giving time
for the " Josephine " to work in her mind.

" I am sure *I* am perfectly willing to drop the
matter," said Mrs. McChesney in an aggrieved

tone; "but Signor Ferranti shall not come here if *my* wishes are to be consulted."

"I don't see, mother, that his music is any the worse for his being unfortunately married," said Philip; "and, if his explanation is true, I can not see any just ground for withholding our hospitality. But we should all consider it wrong to make you uncomfortable. We can stand his absence much better than we can your displeasure."

"Well, it is hard to know what to say or think," Mrs. McChesney responded in a mollified tone, evidently due to this deft tribute to her authority.

"You are all troubling yourselves unnecessarily. Signor Ferranti will not be here again," broke in Flora brusquely and harshly as she left the room.

CHAPTER X.

FLORA'S prediction proved true. Before the evening of the next weekly rehearsal of the quartet Mr. McChesney received the following note :

" MY DEAR Mr. McCHESNEY : I am suffering from a severe attack of congestion of the lungs. I would like to see you, and I therefore ask you as a favor to kindly call at my boarding-house as soon as convenient.

"Very sincerely, yours,

"GIULIO FERRANTI.

"No. 9 WOODLAND AVENUE."

Mr. McChesney wasted no time in obeying this summons. The same afternoon on which he had received the note he mounted the shabby steps and stood on the narrow stoop of one of those high, ungainly, dry-goods-box structures that money-making butchers and keepers of beer-saloons are wont to put up in country towns. These structures may smother the sense of the beautiful in form among the middle classes, but that will

not disturb the mind of the owner. Verily, no;
so that he could get one per cent more for his
investment he would willingly, gladly, sweep all
budding Raphaels, Murillos, and Da Vincis from
the surface of the earth. The suburban town is
unluckily a haven of refuge for the inartistic,
cheap-John landlord who plants his foot against
the wheel of progress. He is not in good odor in
the larger cities, for their architects and builders
recognize well the facts that beauty is not incom-
patible with economy, and that a Queen Anne front
or a Gothic window will cover a multitude of
deficiencies to the house-hunter of æsthetic mind.
Mr. McChesney gave a shudder as he looked up
at the straight façade, unrelieved by a single win-
dow-cap or tasteful projection. The warm sun
brought out severely the smudgy drawings left by
the wet-fingered storm, and the faded pinkish
streaks upon the red window shades which diversi-
fied the sickly yellow of the long-since painted
front. A dingy maid-servant, with open mouth
and a wisp of hair drooping at right angles toward
her shoulder, came to the door and declared that
the "third-floor back" could see no one, "not
even his own mother—he was that sick." Mr.
McChesney insisted on sending up his card. She
reluctantly mounted the stairs, at the head of
which she soon appeared again with the statement,
"He says you kin git up," delivered in a subdued,

confidential whisper, accompanied by a series of patronizing nods.

Mr. McChesney made his way around the sharp corners of one of those dark narrow hallways which economically utilize every inch of room at the expense of light and cheerfulness and comfort, and, after a temporary difficulty with two belligerent steps, invisible in the semi-darkness, he reached Ferranti's room. The signor was lying upon a lounge in front of a small open grate in which feebly burned a few knotty sticks of wood; he made an ineffectual attempt to sit up as Mr. McChesney entered.

" Do not rise, I beg of you," said the latter hastily; " it is not at all necessary. I am sorry to see you looking so ill," he continued, holding Ferranti's hand and noting the thin, flushed face and heavy eyes. " How did you happen to come down so suddenly?"

" Some carelessness during these damp, chill evenings, I suppose," answered Ferranti. " The ubiquitous ego doesn't always assert itself at the right time. I don't know, though, that I should say *the* ego when we all of us seem to have two, one occupied with abstract questions and the other with material matters. Sometimes one dominates us and sometimes the other. The sensible man seems to be the one who compels his two egos to live in peace and harmony, who doesn't allow either one to gain supremacy above the other."

"I quite agree with you, excepting the 'all of us,'" Mr. McChesney replied. "Two thirds of us, poor mortals that we are, can only claim the Philistine ego. We are like the well-fed citizen of Goslar who tells Heine that trees are green because green is good for the eyes. And if some sympathetic Heine agrees with us and assures us in return that the Lord has made cattle because beef soup strengthens man, and that jackasses are created for the purpose of serving as comparisons, and that man exists so that he may eat beef soup and realize that he is no jackass—well, then, we, too, are sensibly moved, and go on our way rejoicing."

Ferranti smiled and said :

"It is considerate of you to say we."

"Yes, yes," Mr. McChesney went on rather hastily. "The trail of the serpent is over us all to a greater or less degree. It takes a good many small atoms to make a perfect being. And, after all, this lumpishness of the beef-eater serves as a good balance-wheel to hold erratic pendulums in place. Still, I confess my weakness; I can't quite cure myself of a desire to kick a stupid man."

"And I confess that I have sometimes a desire to kick myself," Ferranti said.

Mr. McChesney had drawn a chair to the side

of the lounge, and with a sort of womanish tenderness he now adjusted the pillows behind Ferranti's head and spread the afghan smoothly over
him. Presently Ferranti said:

"I have sent for you, Mr. McChesney, because
I feel that I ought to prove the falsity of Kalinski's
assertion. I owe it to you, and in fact I owe it
to myself to do so. Here is the key to the closet
over there; and if I may trouble you to bring me
the two caskets you will find there—"

Mr. McChesney went to the corner of the
room, and, as directed, brought to Ferranti two caskets, one of sandal wood with quaint silver clasps,
and the other of ivory curiously inlaid with
mother-of-pearl and gold. While Ferranti unlocked them and began to examine the papers
which he took from the casket with silver bands,
Mr. McChesney looked around the room with
some curiosity. It revealed a refined taste and
the habits of a luxurious past battling with and
baffling the commonness of poverty. The furni-
ture was cheap and ordinary; the floor was covered with matting, not altogether spotless or in
good repair, but it was partly concealed by three
tiger - skin rugs; the windows were hung with
soft yellow silken draperies, through which shone
a mellow autumnal light; over a shabby, square
deal table was thrown a dark velvet cover, elabo-
rately embroidered; and on the chintz - covered

couch was spread an afghan of Persian colors
blended as harmoniously as the leaves of one of
our Northern autumn forests in late October. The
spaces each side the shallow chimney had been
filled with pine shelves; and on one side stood
the works of the great composers in handsome
dark bindings, while on the other appeared vol-
umes of the philosophers and poets mingled with
psychological works, old and new. Above the
mantel a dark blue cloth had been stretched to
the ceiling, and on it were arranged a number of
swords, rapiers, daggers, poniards, stilettos, together with an Arabian cimeter, a Scotch clay-
more, and a Mexican bowie-knife. A handsome
sword with damaskeened blade and jeweled han-
dle drew an exclamation of interest from Mr.
McChesney, and he walked across the room to
consider it more closely.

Ferranti glanced up from the package of papers he was examining, now and then pulling out
one in a woman's handwriting—

"That sword," he said, "belonged to my father. He was a great traveler in his day, and
made quite a collection of weapons. I carry a few
about with me, more to remind me of him than
from any special interest in them."

"This workmanship is extremely fine," said
Mr. McChesney.

"Yes; the sword was given to my father by

the Sultan of Turkey, to whom he rendered some little service. It has more artistic than murderous merit, I imagine, though."

" I wish that could be said of all our weapons of warfare," Mr. McChesney quickly remarked. " What an absurdity for human beings to kill each other instead of learning to adjust their difficulties by moral means! We are a long way yet from civilization, if we use the word in its right sense."

" I shall be glad," said Ferranti grimly, " when the underlying spirit of Christian law really gets to the surface. So far, in the questions that come up for settlement between nations, we are theoretically altruists, but practically Zulus."

As Mr. McChesney sat down again Ferranti laid his papers by his side and unlocked the other casket. It proved to be merely an outer covering for a blue velvet jewel-case enlaced with gold filigree. From this he took a folded paper which he handed to Mr. McChesney. It was a marriage certificate, attesting in due form the marriage of Anita Bartolomeo to Giulio Ferranti at the Church of Santa Maria in Via.

Mr. McChesney handed it back with the words: " This is quite unnecessary, Signor Ferranti; I am convinced of Kalinski's—mistake—to give him the benefit of every possible doubt."

" But it is as well to make assurance doubly sure," said the signor in return, smiling sadly and replacing the paper in the jewel case, from which shone a sudden glitter of diamonds as the lid was raised and lowered. "These letters," continued he, "were written by my mother," and he gave Mr. McChesney those he had selected from the package. "Please read passages indicated by pencil marks. My boy is under the care of a nurse, and lives in a cottage near my mother's home. She sees him nearly every day."

The first passage read by Mr. McChesney ran as follows, in Italian:

"I saw little Luigi this morning. He grows finely and bids fair to become the image of you when you were a boy. Padre Girolomo declares he will be a poet, he is so intoxicated with delight at the roses now in full bloom. He will lie under the big rose tree that fills the southeast corner of the garden wall and look contentedly at the blue sky for an hour, which is certainly a long time for a boy of five to keep still."

Another passage was: "Luigi is so full of mischief. To-day he wound the kitten up in a sort of harness made of the bright-colored worsteds he had stolen from my work-basket; and yesterday he insisted upon helping old Paolo in the garden. He dulled the best hoe against the stones, and 'weeded up,' as he said, a bed of the crisp young lettuce Paolo is preparing for market."

Still another: "The boy has little recollection

of you, and none at all, I am happy to say, of his
unfortunate mother. Oh, my son, when I think
of your wrecked happiness, of all that you have
endured through that woman, I am tempted to
forget my religion and rebel at the injustice of
your position."

Other passages, which in spite of Mr. McChesney's remonstrances he was compelled to read,
spoke of " Anita " as " no better," as " more quiet,
so the doctors tell me," as having made, " since I
wrote before, a violent and nearly successful attempt at suicide "; or, " better, with one quite lucid
interval last week," and so on, with many details
of home life, and everywhere glimpses of the
sympathy and tenderness of a refined, educated
woman for her absent son. Here and there were
references to money sent which had been laid out
to good advantage for Anita's comfort or Luigi's
benefit, or to keep the cottage household in good
order. Mr. McChesney could not fail to be touched
by these letters, and by the spirit which prompted
the Italian to insist upon his reading them.

" I need not say that your confidence in me is
entirely appreciated," remarked Mr. McChesney,
while Ferranti relocked the caskets.

" And I am very sorry that I can not just now
tell you my reasons for remaining silent in regard
to my real name and position. It will only be a
few months, I believe, before I can write to you

all that I feel bound to conceal now; and, while
all the shadows can not be lifted entirely from my
past, you will at least learn that I have not been,
and am not now, unworthy of your hospitality and
your friendship. I shall probably see you no more,
unless you come to bid me good-by, for I have decided to accept a good offer to travel in South
America. This spring dampness is having a bad
effect upon my lungs; and as others are dependent
upon me I recognize the necessity of taking care of
my health."

"But you will take dinner with us once more?"
Mr. McChesney asked, rashly forgetful of his wife's
last positive command when he left the house.

"Pardon me; I think not. My preparations
will take some little time and—well—the past has
been called back so vividly that I do not feel equal
to saying a verbal good-by to your family. My
visits to your house have been sunny breaks in the
anxieties which beset me, but it is better now, I
think, to send my adieus through you."

A few warm words of regret from Mr. McChesney, and the two men parted; one to resume as
usual his life of leisurely, inoffensive comfort, the
other to break away as quickly as possible from an
enthralling love which was gradually undermining
his reasoning powers and his sense of honor. Ferranti knew only too well that after the noble dignity with which Flora had asserted her confidence

in him, he could not see her again without falling
upon his knees before her and crying out his need
of the love that he sometimes wildly whispered to
himself belonged to him, was the birthright of
which he had been cruelly defrauded. The rever-
ence of a child for the Madonna; the appreciation
of an artist for an artist; the love of a man for a
woman; the sense of possession, of the power of a
strong masculine will over the gentler feminine
will; the knowledge of the barriers that stood between them—all struggled in his mind, like op-
posing waves tossing him hither and thither over
the ocean of thought, until worn out by his con-
tending emotions he lost the power to sleep and
would lie all night in wide-eyed, helpless exhaus-
tion. As the time came nearer for his departure
his strong will reasserted itself. He determined
to pack his books and other belongings and to sail
upon the appointed day. At first the remedy of
mechanical work gave him some relief from his
torturing misery; but his frame was already too
weakened to endure any physical exertion. He
rapidly grew worse and succumbed to an attack of
typhoid fever. The fever lasted nearly two
months. During this time he was visited almost
daily by Mr. McChesney or Philip, and even by
Karl Klinder, who puffed his way up the narrow
stairs to shake his head ominously at the thin face
and burning eyes of the sick man. These were

the only visitors allowed in the room, although
many of the inhabitants of Medalhurst offered
kindly help—forgetting all their past suspicion in
present sympathy.

One day Philip took a bunch of flowers to the
sick man.

"Flora sent them—my sister sent them to
you," he whispered, bending over the pillow.

Ferranti opened his eyes languidly, and motioned that they should be put on the pillow near
him. All that afternoon he rested quietly, now
and then turning his head to inhale the dewy
freshness of the blossoms; but hot thoughts were
rushing through his brain. That night he was in
a wild delirium. What maddening fancies gal-
loped like iron-hoofed horses through his aching
head! Now these pink roses became the soft
pink cheeks whose bloom he had so longed to
touch; and these rich red roses—did they not
hold the sweetness of the lips so far beyond his
reach? and the tall white lilies—there was the
stately full white throat rising from shoulders of
snowy whiteness; and the fragrance of the jas-
mine stars that floated out to his nostrils was it
not the warm, sweet breath of his beloved? His
beloved! no other's, for cold as they might call
her he knew the hidden fire that smoldered beneath her quiet pansy-hued eyes. Cold, did they
call her cold, his stately darling? He could warm

her with the fire of his caresses. He who could check and control himself to win her by the force of higher laws, he could show her, and he only, the warm human love that should bind them closer and closer in the passion of eternal love. And then he dreamed of the cool ferns which she had plucked from the mossy banks along a sparkling brook. He would take her—he would fly with her away from these puny offsprings of a northern clime, and amid the tropic glories of the south he would whisper the glowing words that he had choked down and buried in this icy atmosphere. He gave wild shrieks of delight as he figured to himself the hopeless task of tearing her from his enclasping arms. There were demons in those flowers, and he called on them by fantastic names to fly to his assistance when he bore her—her, his love, his life, his soul, away, away, away!

So imagination, uncontrolled by reason, dragged Ferranti hither and thither, through scenes of ecstasy and through scenes of torture; through dreams of the past and then on to dreams of the future; but ever and again his frenzied fancy circled back to the flowers which he confounded with his beloved. All attempt to remove the flowers but redoubled his delirium. That night four men could scarcely hold him. For days thereafter he hovered between life and death. But the vital force was not yet exhausted. Slowly he came back to life, slowly and surely he recovered strength. It was, however, only a poor, weak image of his former self that struggled one day out into the warm sunlight and the mild April air spiced with budding lilacs. And it was with sad faces that Mr. McChesney and Philip, and a few acquaintances whom Ferranti cared for, went with him to the steamer, a week later, and watched him sail away to fulfill the engagements he refused to break.

CHAPTER XI.

DURING the year that followed Ferranti's departure, the McChesneys lived quietly, as usual, holding themselves somewhat aloof from the imitative routine of city life that characterized Medalhurst, but keeping thoroughly in harmony with the literary and musical atmosphere of the time. Occasionally they would entertain some notable guest, but for the most part they preferred to enjoy without restraint the luxurious freedom of an almost ideal country life. It is, when one thinks of it, a saving grace of humanity that the better portion of it loves the quiet of the country. Even if the stimulus of the city is needed by an artist or a poet to develop his creative powers, or by a business man to arouse his capacity for work, still there lurks in the background of his mind an appreciative fondness for what has been created incapable of sin; a love for the sturdy, straightforward trees, the cheerful, charitable grass, the brilliant free-growing flowers in field and wood, the crystalline purity of the wandering brook, and the thunderous majesty of the flying torrent; and by this love he proves himself worthy of Him in whose image he was made; so that whether he call himself pantheist, theist, Christian, or agnostic, he is by this token part and parcel of the good warring eternally with the powers of evil.

One afternoon in the middle of May, when June seemed to laughingly peep through interlacing young green elm. leaves and pink-flushed apple boughs, Flora was seized with the restlessness that pervades the atmosphere of awakening summer. She could not adapt herself to her wonted occupations, and, taking her garden hat wreathed around with a spray of wild roses, she wandered through the grounds. Though her cheeks were paler than the year before she had not grown less lovely through her sorrow, and in the soft blue dress she wore she seemed a fitting expression of the delicate, misty beauty of the day.

Dreamily she noted the many signs of advancing summer—the clusters of dark-blue violets shadowing the bright green of the fresh-grown grass; the yellow dandelions starring the pathway at either side and shining under long rows of Norway pines, as yellow lamp-lights shine along a country street on some o'erclouded night; the thousand furry catkins bursting to variegated beauty along the upward-pointing branches of the seaside willows; a bed of tulips and yellow daffodils and overscented jonquils, flashing as they swayed to

and fro under the warm breeze like the jewels of an
Eastern queen. A robin sang gayly in the branches of a knotted oak where her nest was being built.
It was a day for love and happiness, and Flora as
she slowly rambled through the fields bitterly re-
proached herself for her discontent. "Why can
I not be happy?" she asked herself. "Am I so
weak and childish that I must have all I wish in
order to be cheerful? Have I no work to do, no
mission to accomplish, no return to make for the
gift of life and the gift of eyes to see the beauty of
the world, that I must cry like a sickly child for a
treasure beyond my reach?" She walked for several hours, now and then sitting down to rest under
some leafy tree through whose overhanging branches she could see the peaceful sky that bent its soothing gaze upon her as a mother glances downward
at a fretting child. But in spite of Flora's efforts
to hold herself in sympathy with the cheerful life
about her, she grew more and more unhappy. The
image of Ferranti was constantly before her eyes;
now grave and melancholy as he would sit before
beginning to play, now radiant with the fire of
genius as he became absorbed in the glorious harmonies of the master composers he loved.

When she went slowly up the sweeping grav-
eled walk that led to the house, she saw her father
sitting upon the broad piazza. He was comforta-
bly reading the evening papers and smoking at the

same time a long pipe. She went up to him and
put one arm over his shoulder with a gentle, caressing motion.

. "Papa, dear," said she, "I feel as if something
were about to happen. I can not shake off the
impression."

Her father looked a moment into her troubled
eyes, then rose, threw down his paper, and took
his pipe out of his mouth.

"Well," said he quizzically, "something *is* going
to happen. The dinner bell is going to ring in a
few minutes; and after you have shaken the dust
from the hem of your garments and smoothed your
haloish locks, you are going to exchange your pre-
sentiment for pie—a game pie, too—one of those
fascinating, but indigestible pies that will take you
back to old English romances and remind you of
Emerson. You know what he said on his Western
trip to a man who constantly refused pie: 'Why,
Mr. B——! What is pie for?'"

"I think I ought to know that story, for I was
the one who told it to you, or rather read it to you.
I don't care for second-hand jokes greatly myself."

"You consider this one pi–racy, eh?" said Mr.
McChesney gravely. Flora shrugged her shoulders and ran up-stairs, while Mr. McChesney, satis-
fied to have banished for the moment her troubled
look, shook his head thoughtfully as he put
away his pipe.

At dinner Flora seemed to have quite recovered her cheerfulness. Afterward she went into the music room. Mr. McChesney followed, took out his viola, and began to tune it in a leisurely way while he walked with slow and measured steps up and down the room. As Flora sat down to the piano she shivered two or three times with uncontrollable nervousness. The soft, warm wind blew in at the open window and with a sudden gust swayed the silken fringe of the lamp-shades and ruffled the light curls on her forehead.

" I think we shall have a storm to-night," said her father, stopping by the front window to look out into the sky, where the lingering tints of a bright sunset were disappearing under mounting piles of gloomy vapor.

Flora ran her fingers lightly over the keys. Suddenly she stopped and spoke to her father, who was occupied with a refractory string.

" Father, something has happened. Signor Ferranti is coming." Saying thus, she arose and walked hesitatingly to the middle of the room as if uncertain whether to go or stay.

Mr. McChesney started and turned toward the door. No one was there and no sound could be heard. He listened for a few moments, then snapped a string impatiently. A rapid footstep was heard upon the gravel walk, the old-fashioned bell sounded a sharp, quick peal, and in a mo-

8

ment Ferranti's voice was heard through the open
door.

He came in carrying his violin-case in his hand.
He was browner and stouter than he had ever
appeared before, and he seemed to radiate an atmosphere of singular vivacity. His eyes sparkled.
He greeted Flora gently, whispering something
softly under his breath as he bent over her hand.
She did not hear the words, but she felt that in
them he had breathed a lingering caress, and that
in the firm clasp of his hand, he had expressed a
confidence and a hope. He had moreover about
him that unmistakable generous air which betokens
a man ready to embrace the whole world—the
poor, wicked, world, that only gets its sins forgiven
now and then in toto by the man who sees a dream
of happiness take shape before him.

Owing to Flora's uncanny announcement Mr.
McChesney shook hands with Ferranti in a somewhat puzzled fashion, and then asked with some
energy : " But—but—where did you come from so
unexpectedly ? You drop in upon us like a—an
angel unawares."

" It is very good of you to imply that I drop
from heaven, but it happens I come from a less
celestial region. I am straight from Valparaiso. I
reached New York this morning, and came out
here at once ; for I had a double purpose in coming." Here he hesitated. Flora made a slight

movement to leave the room, but Signor Ferranti, with a stately courtliness, took her by the hand and led her to a chair by which, when she was seated, he remained standing, one hand resting lightly on the high carved back.

"However and whyever you came, you are certainly welcome," Mr. McChesney said cordially, seeing that his guest was still unready to speak. "I only hope you have missed us half as much this winter as we have missed you. I find to my sorrow that I had learned to depend upon one patient listener to my theories and speculations. I hope your stay here will not be a short one."

"A very short one, I fear. A letter has been following me from place to place for two months, and it only overtook me at Valparaiso. I canceled all engagements, and left for New York by the first steamer; for the letter informed me—of the death of my unfortunate wife. She died about three months ago at the asylum where she was confined. By a singular coincidence, I received at the same time a letter from my mother, announcing the death of her only brother about a month ago at Rome. On account of his death it is necessary for me to return to Italy at once. My principal reason in coming out here to-day is "—and again Ferranti hesitated—" to—well—to ask your permission to tell your daughter of my love for her and to ask her to become my wife."

This second surprise proved almost too much for Mr. McChesney. He recklessly dropped his fiddle-bow and sat down upon the nearest chair. He had considered that Signor Ferranti's interest in the McChesney family was purely a musical and literary interest in which Hugh McChesney himself proved the pivot around which Ferranti's thoughts revolved. Mr. McChesney did not pick up his bow, but folded his arms resignedly.

Ferranti continued, his voice growing more impassioned : " It was impossible for me to help loving her. Since the first moment I saw her she has been to me the realization of the ideal which haunted me in my music and ever fluttered above me on heavenly wings, mocking my loneliness and proving at once my solace and my despair. I did not think my aspirations would ever be gratified. I dared not hope to enter the lists with others that I might prove the depth and sincerity of my adoration. I tried neither by word nor look to betray myself. I would not, if I could help it, hint of my longing love while under this cloud of unhappiness that has smothered me—held me in a vice which has made it impossible sometimes to draw a free long breath ; and though there might seem a law of justice that would free me from the burden of a clanking chain about my neck, I dared not insult the purity of a noble woman by asking her to link her name with one who, however inno-

cent himself, must bear the stigma of divorce.
But I felt sometimes that the subtle mysterious
current that runs from heart to heart, and that
pulses through the harmonies of the music we have
played together, must indicate my love, my sorrow,
my repression. I am free now to say to her what I
wish. May I speak to her?" And he drew a labored
breath. Mr. McChesney did not look up or speak.

With a tremor in his voice, Ferranti continued:
" My haste would seem unpardonable—but, I have
waited so long. I must, as I said before, return at
once to Italy, and I can not remain here, I—can
not stay in the same house with her without knowing whether I may waken to a new life or sleep
again in the dullness of cold endurance."

There was a curious little downward droop of
bitterness in Mr. McChesney's smile as he answered : " But in America we get the daughter's
consent before we ask the father's. You will have
to consult my daughter. I shall not stand in the
way of her happiness if it is to be assured in this
way. You shall talk with her." He looked kindly
at his daughter as he spoke, but his step was not
light, nor his movement brisk as he put aside the
silken hangings and passed into the hall.

.   .   .   .

Oh that golden moment when two are alone conscious of their mutual love and conscious for the
first time that all obstacles to its expression are

removed! Ferranti's face grew pale with intense
emotion as he approached Flora. He saw that
her hazel eyes were suffused with unshed tears
when she put her hand in his with trembling confidence. He drew her closer and closer to him in
a silent embrace born of peace and of the perfect
love which purifies all passion and lifts men and
women to kinship with the angels. How well
this moment repaid the nervous tension, the weary
strain of endurance of the past slow-dragging year!
A shower of liquid Italian words, dropping from
his lips, broke the stillness as gently as the downward flutter of a thousand ripe rose petals breaks
the quiet of the southern summer night.

Swiftly passed the moments of love and silence and happiness and murmuring words. The
hurrying shadows gradually filled the room, the
light faded from the evening sky; a sudden wind
swished up from the west and clashed the tree-tops
together with that hissing energy which marks the
prelude to a thunder-storm; the blinds slammed
to and fro, and soon the rain-drops, driven against
the window-panes, sounded a tinkling treble and
a droning base to the irregular ryhthmic accent of
the surging winds. Neither Ferranti nor Flora,
occupied as they both were with their own thoughts
and with the low-toned broken words that half expressed emotion, paid attention to the storm until
a vivid lightning flash lit up the room and simul-

taneously a crashing thunder-clap burst above
them, as if Jupiter Pluvius himself would so express a disapproval of too much mortal happiness.

Flora rang for lights. When she sat down
again Ferranti smoothed back her golden hair and
asked her a whispered question. She turned her
face to his in amazement, as she said: "What!
play the Rubinstein sonata; now, and here? How
can you ask it?"

"Why not, my darling? It is time your fears
were set at rest. We must be one in soul; if there
is any lingering shadow of disturbance in your
mind, let us drive it away now."

Flora still looked at him wonderingly, but she
arose and placed the music on the piano. When
all was ready Ferranti came over to the piano and
stood by her as he had stood so many times before.
With the hesitation of true affection he had re-
frained from kissing her lips, though he had
snatched a thousand kisses from her hands, her
hair, and her flushed cheeks. He bent now above
her, drew back her head, and calling her for the
first time by her name, said:

"Flora, carissima, are you afraid of me?"

Mastered by the fiery splendor of those brilliant
forceful eyes, Flora felt all minor thoughts disap-
pear as stubble before a fire. "No, not afraid,"
she murmured. "I know that I love you. I
know too that you are the only one who can bend

me to your will. But had you ten times the power that I know you must possess, still I would trust you. I am willing to lose my identity in yours; I am no more myself—I am you." And the swift color swept in waves from her white neck to her delicately veined forehead, though she did not drop her clear blue-gray eyes.

The great wave of feeling that rose from Ferranti's heart blurred his eyes and chilled his hands. He remained very quiet however, looking long into the sweet womanly face uplifted to his; and his voice was husky when he said :

"So do I reverently take your dear heart and life and soul into my keeping."

Then, and for the first time, he pressed a kiss upon her lips. And there came over him a mighty quiver, like that which shook the strong trees by the window, and he raised himself with an effort, and seizing his violin bow looked downward at the rose-red face of her whom he loved. "So small you are, so dainty and so sweet," he whispered, "and yet I tremble at *your* power." Then he began the sonata, and invested with newer, richer meaning the harmonics bore the lovers away upon

> The tides of music's golden sea
> Setting toward eternity.

Faith and love illuminated Flora's face. Would the restless spirit of the past be conquered?

CHAPTER XII.

In the mean time Mr. McChesney had gone to hunt for his wife. After vainly searching through every room, he found her in one corner of the garden back of the house, where she was superintending the work of planting a young Chinese magnolia. A fresh odor rose from the rich brown earth, and the grass and flowers seemed to hold themselves upright in anxious expectation of the coming rain. Mr. McChesney sniffed the grateful moisture in the air.

"My dear," said he, "hadn't you better come in? It is going to rain."

"Yes, I know it; but the house is not far away."

"I have something to tell you—the gardener can do that alone."

"Wait till this is done; I want to see it done properly. Why can't you tell me here?" steadying the top of the bush as she spoke.

"It is too important."

"Well, it can't be important enough for me to leave this. I bought it myself this afternoon; and it is just the right time to set it out before a storm." She proceeded to adjust with her own fingers some delicate root-tendrils, and received thereby a shower of dirt on her hands from the spade of the unobserving gardener.

"There! your ruffles are spoiled," said Mr. McChesney.

"Well, my temper isn't, any way," said she, calmly wiping her soiled hands on a dainty embroidered handkerchief.

Mr. McChesney turned away and paced steadily up and down the broad asphaltum walk, until the stout little lady made a flushed but triumphant appearance at his side. Then he took her possessively under one arm and walked her quickly into the library.

"What is your important news?" she asked, taking up a palm-leaf fan and using it energetically.

Mr. McChesney walked two or three times around the room and then gazed reflectively out of the window. Mrs. McChesney, used to his ways, waited until he had apparently studied to his heart's content each separate tree on the lawn; then—

"Hugh! Hugh!" she said; "why don't you say what you want to?"

"Well, I hardly think my news will suit you, my dear."

"It certainly will not suit me any better to have you delay so long in telling it. It generally takes you five hours to get out something that I could say in five minutes." Mrs. McChesney's patience was becoming exhausted.

"Well—m—mmph!"—the latter ejaculation somewhat decisive—"I saw Signor Ferranti this afternoon."

"Did you? Where? What is he doing here, so suddenly?"

"I suppose he has a right to come here, hasn't he? You wouldn't keep him out of the place, would you?" Mr. McChesney shot out these sentences with considerable vigor as he began to realize his latent weakness.

"Perhaps he has and perhaps he hasn't. It's just according to one's point of view."

"He is here in town, and you will probably see him. I hope, for my sake, Josephine, that you will receive him with some show of friendliness."

"When do you expect him?" with ominous quietness.

"Th—er—the fact is, he is here now."

"Here now! And you have sent Flora to entertain him! I never saw such a man! Are you crazy, Hugh McChesney?" And she started forward as if to leave the room.

"Wait, wait, a moment," said her husband with outward bravery if with some inward trepidation:

"Your objection to married men does not avail any more—his wife is dead." And Mr. McChesney, conscious that his sympathies were with the lovers, bent a smiling, antagonistic gaze upon his wife.

"Oh, that is enough!" said Mrs. McChesney, sinking back in her chair and clicking her fan sharply against a table by her side.

Mr. McChesney was agreeably surprised. He had quite expected an hysterical outburst. But Mrs. McChesney continued: "That means that he will ask Flora to marry him—a poor violinist, a concert player, a—"

"But an artist and a gentleman," interrupted her husband. "Besides, she may refuse him."

"Refuse him! I think, Hugh, you have more penetration than the rest of your sex—but—I pity the rest of them. Did you ever know a woman to refuse the man she really cared for when she could accept him, excepting in some three-volume English novel. No," she continued, sighing, "she will not refuse him; I saw the possibilities a year ago. Oh, Hugh! what can be done?"

"If she loves him, dear, there is nothing to be done but for us to make the best of it," said Mr. McChesney with commonplace philosophy.

"But you are glad to make the best of it and I am not. Of course it is easy for you to philosophize. Oh I can not bear it, I can not! My beautiful child! she might grace a palace!" Then

Mrs. McChesney put her head upon the corner of the table and began to cry softly.

Her husband kissed the smooth brown hair streaked with gray and put his arm about the rounded waist, once as slender as her daughter's. They had never entirely outgrown their lover-like ways, these staid married people. It is true they had their little tiffs and jarrings now and then; but the tiffs and jarrings were only motes in the sunbeam of affection that lighted their journey through life. He comforted her now, therefore, with many consoling words, adding at last:

"I have never told you all I learned about Signor Ferranti when I called upon him after Kalinski's dramatic outburst. I will tell you what I suspect if you will listen."

After a lengthy conversation, during which Mrs. McChesney grew more composed, Mr. McChesney suggested that they should go to the music room. When they reached the doorway of the library they heard the opening strains of the Rubinstein sonata.

"What are they playing that thing for?" Mr. McChesney jerked out angrily.

"I think so, too," his wife said vaguely. "If she has any *more* hallucinations she shall never marry him—*never*," dabbing her eyes viciously with her husband's handkerchief. "I believe he has bewitched us all, any way; he deals in the

black arts, I am sure; a lineal descendant of—
Machiavelli," she continued, bravely fishing an
Italian name from the chaotic deep of memory.

"Cagliostro, my dear, Cagliostro," said her husband.

"Well, it doesn't make much difference.
The old Italians I have read of were very much
alike. We never hear of the stupid men, and
the bright men were all consumed with melancholy or cynicism or superstition."

Mr. McChesney opened his mouth to confute
this feminine logic, but the door-bell rang and
Karl Klinder stepped in.

"There fall some water-drops," said he. "I
wass going py and I stop until the rain is ofer;
should I?" addressing Mrs. McChesney.

"Yes, indeed; of course," she answered. And
she directed the maid to carry away his dripping
hat and coat.

"Do I hear the violin of Signor Ferranti?" he
asked with surprise. "Wo kommt er nun? It is
he, nicht wahr?" excitedly relapsing into German.
"Ach! the esteemable man! It rejoices me much
him to see once more again. He is love-worthy.
You will rejoice, too, him to see again?" to Mrs.
McChesney.

"He has come a long distance," she answered,
begging the question, "from South America—Valparaiso, I believe."

"So?" said Klinder. "And he play dot Rubinstein sonata once more, once more ahgén."

"Shall we go in?" said Mr. McChesney addressing his wife.

"No; let us sit here until they are through playing."

She threw herself as she spoke on the huge brass-nailed sofa that ran along one side of the square front hall; Mr. McChesney followed her example; while Klinder seated himself opposite, his rotund figure contrasting with the severe dignity of the straight, high-backed chair he had chosen, and from which his pudgy feet could scarcely reach the floor.

As the players began the third movement of the sonata, the subdued excitement of the listeners showed itself in different ways. Mrs. McChesney twisted a handkerchief around her forefinger. Mr. McChesney folded his arms with scornful resignation, Karl Klinder took off his spectacles and solemnly blinked his eyes.

A first, a second, a third time the expected phrase appeared. On swept the sonata in strong purpose and fiery freedom. For once the climax was reached without failure, and the closing chords rang out unmarred. The Rubicon was passed. Ferranti drew a long breath, heard in the hall.

"Miss Flora is no longer witt the countenance

worrited; he is outgone," said Klinder, beaming at Mrs. McChesney.

"Bosh!" Mr. McChesney ejaculated. "That face was only the result of imagination or indigestion."

"Now, Hugh; you are certainly mistaken. Depend upon it, there was some association, connected with the sonata, that brought *her* face to his mind when he played. A strong sympathy exists between him and Flora. I saw it the first time they played together."

"Yes, that is true; and the whole thing could be explained, if you choose, on the theory of hypnotic influence; but I can't think Flora has so weak a will."

"No, that isn't it, Hugh. It is no more strange that she should see the face visible to him than that she should anticipate the manner in which he was to render a coming musical thought; no more strange, indeed, than that I should sometimes catch the very words from your lips before you speak. It is no more strange to *me* than a thousand other mysterious things to which we are so used that we take no notice of them. Why does the thought of an absent friend flash suddenly upon the mind a few moments before he unexpectedly arrives? Look at remarkable dreams! There was that dream of mine last—"

Mr. McChesney rose hastily. "There, there,

my dear; I admit that there is considerable truth
in what you say, but excuse me from any dream
theories. It is easy enough to trace dreams back
to their developing cause. As this curious face-
appearance is a troublesome subject, let us keep it
in the background in future," and he looked at
Klinder, who nodded sympathetically.

"I am sure *I* should never dream of mention-
ing it; but some day you will find I am right
about it." A perceptible note of conscious mar-
tyrdom vibrated through Mrs. McChesney's words.
Mr. McChesney smiled indulgently, as the best of
men are wont to smile at the woman who unites
in herself intuitive logic, keen perception, and a
childish unreasonableness—a combination which
renders the woman in whom it occurs at the same
time the most fascinating and certainly the most
exasperating of created beings.

CHAPTER XIII.

THE next day Signor Ferranti had an interview with Mr. and Mrs. McChesney. At his request the two caskets which he had left with Mr. McChesney to care for during his absence were brought to him. He put them on the table before him and left them unopened while he spoke. He began in a low and earnest voice, and he addressed himself at first entirely to Mrs. McChesney.

"I only wish I could take your daughter with me to Italy while she is still ignorant of the fact that I am anything more than a poor violinist, depending upon my own exertions for a living. She loves me for myself"—his face brightened to a smile of exceeding happiness—"and there is no thought in her mind of material good. Thank God, I have it in my power to recompense her noble affection! But this is not what I wish to say. I feel it necessary to set aside my own somewhat romantic wishes and to give you a full explanation of my present circumstances; because—I must ask your consent to an immediate marriage."

"Impossible! I could not consent to it!" murmured Mrs. McChesney. Ferranti shot a keen glance at her from under half-closed eyelids, and continued: "In these caskets you will find full evidence of my connection with the noble house of Mantini. By the death of my uncle, Duke Fabrizio Ferranti, the family estates and title pass into my hands. Your daughter, I am glad to assure you, will be the Duchess of Mantini." A little sarcastic smile curved the corners of his lips as he noted the quick flush that burned in Mrs. McChesney's face. "With her beauty and accomplishments she will grace the old palace at Rome as no other woman has graced it since the day of the beautiful Duchessa Constanza Maria, who was known throughout all Italy for her noble charities and her keen intelligence, as well as for her exquisite beauty."

A fluttering sigh escaped from Mrs. McChesney's lips. She remained silent however, though her heavy breathing and burning cheeks showed the effect of his words, and she listened attentively while he continued:

"There are some other things I ought to tell you, so that all my past life in its most important particulars may be quite clear to you. I quarreled with my uncle, who lived at Rome, on account of my marriage with the Anita whose picture you have seen. She was young and beautiful, with that devilish kind of beauty that bewitches a boy's senses while it drowns his reason. She became to all appearances passionately attached to me. Impulsively, as I then thought, she constantly compromised herself by throwing herself in my way under peculiar circumstances. Finally, I married her, secretly and under an assumed name. I was twenty and she but seventeen. I thought her, if low-born, at least a model of purity and womanly devotion. I confessed the marriage to my family that in case of my death she might be protected; and I intended then, at all risks, to acknowledge her publicly as soon as my position and means would allow. My uncle cast me off entirely. My mother, though bitterly grieved at my marriage, helped me in every way possible, but as she too was dependent on my uncle, I could accept but little from her. In less than a year Anita became moody and unhappy. She implied that I had deceived her, and that she should cease to love me entirely if I could not give her the rank and position to which she considered herself entitled. I need not weary you with my struggles and trials. I went to Paris, and by means of my musical talent I soon began to earn a fair income, enough to live in comfort if not luxury. But such a life was too quiet for Anita. At the end of the second year of our marriage she ran away with a rich Russian count; she left a heartless letter for me, and she also left behind her a baby boy, ten months old. The child I sent to my mother. I did not follow Anita—I had learned to know her too well; but I kept track of her movements. Deserted by the count, she became associated with a French duke, as low in character as he was high in lineage. She used to drive in the Bois de Boulogne, handsome as an empress and apparently happy, until one day she took small-pox and was carried to the hospital. There I visited her and begged her to return to an honest life ; and I offered then to send her back to her old home and to see that she received as large an income as I could afford to send her. She laughed scornfully at my suggestions, and, possessed with the spirit of evil which had grown steadily beyond her control, when she came out of the hospital she plunged into the lowest depths of Parisian life. She was at length arrested in a violent fit of insanity and taken to the police station. From that place I rescued her and sent her to an asylum, where she was cared for until her death. While, if under any circumstances a divorce would be justifiable, it would be so in mine, I never thought it right to procure one, on account of my family name. I paid no attention to women after this unhappy marriage, and have cared for none—until I saw your daughter."

Ferranti, when he had finished speaking, raised the lid of the larger casket. " Here," said he, "are the jewels that belonged to my mother. She insisted upon my keeping them with me in case of any sudden misfortune that might leave me destitute in a strange land. They will belong to your daughter. I leave them in your hands now, and I hope that she will wear them on her wedding day."

Mrs. McChesney would have been more than woman had she not experienced a sudden sensation of pleasure at the royal glitter of the jewels as Ferranti placed the case in her hands, and less than woman had not her heart been touched by this quiet recital of his troubles.

With quick perception he took advantage of her train of thought. He bent the full power of his glowing eyes appealingly upon her, and said:

"I must go to Italy in one week. You will not compel me to go alone? To leave your daughter? It is hard to ask you to part with her, but you will not subject me to the misery of an unnecessary separation? You have been happy yourself; do not deny me the happiness I need." He placed the casket in her hands as he spoke.

Mrs. McChesney hesitated, but only for a moment. "You have indeed been unhappy," she said gently, "but my daughter's happiness is first in my eyes. If she consents to go with you I—" but her voice broke; she could say no more. A teardrop fell in among the diamonds, a jewel of purer luster than any in the casket for it came from a mother's heart.

Ferranti laid one hand upon hers. "She is my life," he said wistfully. "The matter is in your hands," he continued; "and I do not ask for impossibilities."

And Mrs. McChesney, as she passed out of the room holding the casket, quietly murmured, "It shall be as Flora wishes."

"To you, Mr. McChesney," said Ferranti, "I can only say, that you have been my friend under all circumstances, and you know all that I would say. You have heard the rest of the story that I could not honorably finish before. The business matters I wish to arrange consist mainly in seeing that your daughter's fortune, whatever it may be, shall be settled entirely upon herself and her own children. Luigi, if he lives, will inherit my title and the old Mantini palace; but a part of the property is in my own power, and my uncle's private fortune is left to me unreservedly by a codicil added to his will after he heard of Anita's death. This property I would like to settle in part upon your daughter, if I can do so according to American laws, before she becomes my wife."

CHAPTER XIV.

WHILE preparations for the wedding were going on the good citizens of Medalhurst were agitated to no small degree. Each envious spinster and unmarried belle whispered to herself that "Flora McChesney had an inkling of the truth all the time"; the elderly matron who had sternly put Ferranti in his place as a disguised Jesuit shook her head as she confided to her husband her conviction that Mrs. McChesney was "a deep woman—trust her to procure an eligible parti for her daughter"; while the business men, hearing of the marriage settlements, struggled resolutely to disbelieve that any Italian violinist could be at the same time wealthy, moral, honorable, and sane. "McChesney had better look out," "There may be some trickery in spite of appearances," "I should like to be pretty sure of those documents myself," were some of the sentences that passed between these worthy patriarchs. On the whole, the substratum of unadulterated self-conceit that underlies all other qualities of the human mind at Medalhurst as elsewhere in the world was severely broken up by the cataclysmic news of Flora McChesney's coming marriage. Mothers, husbands, and daughters felt to the uttermost their own capacity to shine as mothers-in-law, fathers-in-law, and wives to any number, of bona-fide Italian dukes—if they had only had the chance. Ah, these good people; how many of them put on the steel armor of suspicion at the approach of one stricken with poverty! How many of them fail to see, through their helmet of distrust, nobility of soul and purity of heart when hidden beneath a melancholy face and a shabby coat! And how suitably are they punished if attacking a " Feathertop " of their own creation they find him (unlike Hawthorne's illusive scarecrow) showing behind his poor habiliments the bones and sinews of a man, who routs them in fair fight upon their chosen field.

Fortunately the aggrieved sense of being cheated soon passed away, obliterated by a mild feeling of self-gratulation; for were not the people of Medalhurst, one and all, part and parcel of a wide-spreading halo soon to surround Strathcarron —a halo which would soon be perceived by the whole civilized republican world?

Philip was the only one of whom people had the opportunity of asking questions, and during his calls and leisurely walks he gave the simple facts unreservedly. One evening, while he was going down the main business street of the town, he felt his arm grasped from behind, and at the same time he smelled a strong odor of liquor from a hot breath against his cheek. Turning around sharply, he saw Kalinski wearing a rusty-brown coat and red neck-tie, and a shabby hat cocked toward one eye. Kalinski, who was in a state of maudlin belligerency, steadied himself with an effort. " Is it true," said he, " that your sister is going to marry that devilish fool Ferranti? "

"It is true that my sister is going to marry Duke Giulio Ferranti of Mantini," answered Philip, gravely.

" Duke Sillio Fiddlesticks," said Kalinski, with an oath, " how he has humbugged you all, and he has destroyed my happiness too, d—n him!" And his face grew still redder, as anger for a moment dominated the effect of whisky.

There had been little intercourse between Philip and Kalinski during the past year; yet the friendship had not entirely ceased, for Philip was warm-hearted, and found it hard to cherish anger toward one whom he pitied even more than he condemned. It would seem, indeed, that men are justly declared to be stronger in their friendships than women, so often do the latter use the stings of gossip and the cold shoulder to push an unfortunate sister still further to destruction, while the former, as a rule, cling tenaciously to ties of boyhood or associations of manhood, and hold out, until the last moment, a friendly hand to the erring brother whom they can not turn from a downward path. Yet one result of this is not altogether satisfactory; for the evil-disposed get more help than they deserve, while the humble, deserving, ambitious good are left to struggle upward alone. That positive work for good is always better than negative no one can deny, although a practical application of this theory often seems momentarily cruel to those who look only at temporary results instead of at the great general progress of humanity. Philip was no exception to the best of his sex. He had gone often to see Kalinski, and had remonstrated with him again and again on his growing fondness for liquor. But all to no avail. Sternly surveying now the seedy figure before him, though a pang of pity shot through his heart, he harshly asked:

"Aren't you man enough yet to give up that stale idea of wrecked happiness? Don't you know yet that a woman in love with one man can not love another—it is foreign to her nature? My sister never had any special feeling for you beyond a friendly interest—never will have, and never could have. You are not her ideal of a man; and at present you do not even deserve my friendship. I forbid you to mention her name in any possible connection with your-

self. If you were in your senses you would see
the nonsense of always harping on the string of
unrequited affection. What absurdity! To waste
your time and brains in brooding over the fact
that a woman can not and will not love you!
There is no such thing as genuine love unless it is
mutual. If your fancied love can not resolve
itself into honest, friendly admiration, you may be
pretty sure you are only suffering from wounded
vanity or, worse yet, from a base, brutal passion of
which you ought to be ashamed."

"Hé bien! you talk well," growled Kalinski,
sullenly. "Mais moi? I burn! I will have revenge upon him," growing excited and slapping
his breast tragically.

"Burn? no wonder, considering the vile stuff
you have been drinking," said Philip.

Kalinski straightened himself, assumed an air
of virtuous dignity, and said in a thick voice:
"Philip McChesney, we have been friends but
now we are enemies—hic—enemies I say. Any
man who says I have been drinking insults—me.
I am a soldier, a man of ho–honor, Philip McChesney. Don't you dare say I've been drinking. But
if I had—what then? The old philosophers drank,
old patriarchs drank, apostles drank; Timothy
said, 'a little wine for the stomach's sake.' Now
I say, 'a little wine for the heart's sake.' But I
never was a drinking man, Philip McChesney.

My heart is breaking, and you—hic—you accuse
me of drinking?" He blinked his red-lidded eyes
and attempted to look reproachfully at Philip.
Then he added, explosively: "No man shall insult
me, d—n it! A man's feelings are his own property, I say."

"I only wish they were in your case," muttered
Philip sotto voce and between his closed teeth.
His expression, however, changed as he continued
to look Kalinski steadily in the face, and he said
very gently:

"I beg your pardon, will you allow me to walk
home with you?"

Kalinski, not to be outdone in politeness made
an erratic, dogged bow, and put his hand on Philip's arm.

"Philip, I always said you were my friend.
We are—hic—more than friends. We are broth-
ers. Nous sommes bons camarades, Philip mon
brave, n'est-ce pas? The world goes against me,
Philip," dropping into a sentimental whine.
"Good by, proud world, I'm going home. I go
with you; I get rid of the world; I go home—but
un verre de vin—one—but one—" As he fumbled
unsteadily in his pocket with one hand, with the
other he tried to pull Philip toward the neighbor-
ing wine shops and beer palaces resplendent in gilt
signs, huge plate-glass windows, and other tokens
of prosperity.

Philip shook his head. "We will go to your rooms, Kalinski," he answered. Kalinski did not resist the persuasive touch. "All right, Philip— Good by, proud world—hic—let's go home." And he patronizingly waved his hand to the bar-rooms as arm in arm with Philip he strode toward his apology for a home.

Philip, however, with all his philosophy, found it not overpleasant to listen all the way to incoherent angry mutterings about "lost star," "dewdrop," "chartreuse," "maraschino," to which Kalinski in turn compared Flora, varying his poetic fragments with occasional curses of Ferranti; and it was with considerable relief that the much-enduring philosopher deposited at last the much-imbibing sciolist vigorously in a large arm-chair. He then stood a few moments in the doorway, and regarded the semi-brutalized man with a glance of mingled pity and disgust. Kalinski, putting on the feeble air of bravado that every tipsy man likes to display, began to whistle. "You had better take a cold shower-bath at once, and see if you can't get a little common sense with it," were Philip's parting words as he shut the door. He went home sick at heart, but forebore to speak of his meeting with Kalinski.

CHAPTER XV.

THE sun shone bright and clear on the morning of the wedding day. The ceremony was to take place, according to English fashion, at twelve o'clock. About ten o'clock Ferranti came to the house to see Philip in regard to some detail forgotten by both, for the best man, an attaché of the Italian legation at Washington, could not arrive in time to perform the usual duties of his position. Ferranti stood talking with Philip at the further end of the hall just back of the staircase, when Flora came down the stairs hastily. He heard the swish of her dress and caught her in his arms, giving a low musical laugh, the first laugh she had ever heard from his lips. He brushed his hand caressingly over the loose morning gown of delicate pinkish gray trimmed with lace, and crumpled the soft silk in his hand.

"I like better to see you in this than in your stiff white wedding dress and diamonds," he said. "You are now like a rose—a damask rose-bud—like the dainty roses that I love and that I will show you in the garden, when we shall sit together and breathe the perfume of the orange blossoms and see the golden globes hanging in the midst of glossy greenness, and watch from the high terrace the silver gray of olive grove and the white square-ness of the gleaming villas melting into the Tyrian purple of the twilight sky; and you, my queen, my beauty, my love, will shake your golden hair about me, bend your hazel eyes to mine, while I kneel at your feet in the odorous darkness. Ah! my happiness is too great! I can not breathe when I think of it!" And his dark eyes shone and his face grew pale and luminous with feeling.

Flora put her soft warm hands over his cold fingers and smoothed back the hair from his fore-head. She was now calmer than he, for in the love of a good woman there always exists some-thing of the mother-feeling toward the man she loves. "I hope we shall be very happy, Giulio," said she, slowly speaking his name for the first time, and turning away while he held her hands in a lingering clasp.

"Hello, Ferranti! Don't go yet a moment," called Philip. "I nearly forgot to say the express-man brought a box for you this morning, and left it here. It is directed here, so I suppose it is a wedding present." Ferranti went back to the lower hall. The box stood on a large square mahogany table; it was about two feet square with an "Adams Express Company" label pasted on

one side and " This side up with care," on the top
in letters of black paint.

" Flowers, perhaps, or china," said Flora,
whose curiosity had led her to follow Ferranti.

" But who would send *me* anything of the kind
now, with this direction," Ferranti said in a low
tone, looking at the neatly written address :—

For Signor Giulio Ferranti,
" Strathcarron,"
Medalhurst,
New Jersey.

" Open it, please," said Flora with emphasis,
putting her hand on his arm while the soft folds
of her dress swept against him.

" Carrissima, how can I, when you are so near
me ? " he whispered, bending back his head to look
in her eyes. " The perfume of your hair intoxi-
cates me. All my senses are steeped in a dream
of delight; I have no command over material
things. I have no room for curiosity ; nor for
any thought save you, my little darling, my—"

Flora smilingly put her hand over his mouth.
He seized it and kissed it with a sudden intensity
of passion that brought the swift color to her
cheeks and caused her to step back half timidly.
Ferranti gave again a low, musical laugh—that
laugh, born of excess of happiness, which is so
rarely heard from human beings, and yet which

should be as natural to us all as the singing of the birds or the bubbling of the mountain streams. He then drew from his pocket a small silver dagger of curious workmanship, one which he always carried about with him, pulled it from its sheath and began to pry up the lid of the box.

During this time Philip had been leaning against the jamb of the large door that opened from the back hall upon a large piazza. The door was open, and through it he could see the indefinable brooding sweetness of the young spring landscape budding into life. The snowy pear trees stood arrayed in bridal beauty and the flushing apple trees dropped their dainty petals on the soft green sward beneath; mingled with their fragrance came the mignonette-like odor from the grape vine clinging to a long old-fashioned arbor. He had been drinking in the morning loveliness and drawing long breaths of the delicious morning air, and now he had turned his head to watch his sister's face with a dreamy intentness, perhaps thinking of the day when a maiden's face he knew should blush for him and he too should tremble at approaching happiness.

When Ferranti inserted his dagger under the box-lid and a first faint crack of the wood was heard, Philip started. As though obeying an uncontrollable impulse, he sprang forward. "Hold! Stop!" he cried, and in an instant he tore the

box from Ferranti's hands and hurled it with all
his force through the open doorway. It cleared
the steps of the broad piazza and struck the paved
walk just under a large elm tree. There was a
sudden explosion, a flash of fire. The fragments
of the box, the branches of the tree, a portion of
the grape arbor covering the walk, pieces of iron
and steel, hustled confusedly through the air.
The panes of glass in the back windows were shivered to fragments; vases and bric-à-brac splintered
on the hard-wood floor of the music room; the
statue of Wagner, jarred from its position, fell forward with a loud discordant clang.

Philip, who nearly lost his balance in throwing
the box, was flung heavily backward through the
open door and measured his full length upon the
floor, where he lay senseless, his head cut open
above one temple and his face covered with blood.
Ferranti had seized Flora by the arm at the sound
of the explosion, and, with a lightning glance at
the possibilities of danger, had swung her out of
the way of a tall silver lamp that wavered on
its pedestal and fell directly where she was standing. Both he and Flora escaped unhurt. An
examination of Philip's wound showed a piece of
iron imbedded in his head, how deeply could not
be told until the arrival of physicians.

A bed was hastily arranged in the music room,
and on it the young, manly figure was laid by his

trembling father and Ferranti. Mrs. McChesney, hastily summoned, beyond the first startled cry said nothing; pale and stern she did everything possible for the comfort of the unconscious one so heedless of her efforts. Her fingers trembled, but her face was calm. She even paused a moment to smooth the hair of the bitterly sobbing Flora, who knelt by the side of her brother and murmured reproaches upon herself and words of piteous entreaty to Philip. The servants gathered sadly in the hall and on the piazza. Philip's manliness and generosity and gentleness had so endeared him to them all that there were none who would not gladly have saved him from danger at the expense of suffering to themselves. With tearful eyes they looked now and then at the sorrowing group, while with light footfalls they cleared away the débris of the explosion. The bright sun flashed in merrily at the windows and lighted the room with its coldly cheerful rays, and the warm spring breeze, scented with the blossom odors, ruffled the hair of the apparently dying man, who, save for an occasional gurgling groan, gave no indication of life.

There was an hour of anxious waiting before the famous specialists upon whose word they depended could arrive. In the mean time local physicians held a consultation, and gave but little hope of Philip's recovery. As gently as possible the terrible probability of speedy death was broken to the family. The mother, brave even now, smiled with divine compassion at her son who, under the influence of restoratives, opened his brown eyes, with an appealing glance at the gentle face bent above his own. " Mother ! " He struggled feebly to express himself, but the internal bleeding choked his utterance, so that the broken words that followed were scarcely caught. " Darling mother—this is harder—for you—than for me. I am not afraid. It is but a little sooner—a few years—may be. Now, listen," and he beckened them all nearer, motioning with his hand to Ferranti. " I can not recover — I know — my throat—my head—but the wedding. It must be —here ; I must see it. You do not know. Send for clergyman — and your wedding dress — the diamonds—"

" My God ! it can not be ! " burst in a groan from the lips of Ferranti. " To take your sister, when through me you have lost your life ! Oh, the horror—the wretchedness of it ! I can not ; it is too much ! " And his face grew stony and gray as he slowly clinched his hands.

Philip turned his eyes from his mother's to his father's face. " Beg him, for my sake— mother ! father ! " he said, with a spasm of energy which brought a gush of blood from his lips and caused him to relapse into unconsciousness.

The father tenderly wiped the pale face and spoke
a few low words to the physician who stood near
noting Philip's pulse. The mother clasped her
hands and stretched both arms slowly outward.
It was her first movement of uncontrollable anguish. Ferranti left the room and began to pace
up and down the long walk in front of the house.
Slowly, minute by minute, the time went by until
the arrival of the two physicians who had been
telegraphed for. Gravely and sympathetically
they made the examination on which the trembling hopes of the family hung quivering. All
waited with beating hearts. No hope?

Oh! who that has heard that gloomy sentence
can fail to remember how it weighs upon the soul,
binds it with leaden gyves, relentlessly smothers
each springing thought of joy, and, like a vam-
pire, sucks the life-blood from the heart till that
pulsing center of delight beats faintly in the dull
despair of so-called resignation! "No hope!"
Bitter words to the girl clinging to the lover who
has betrayed her, yet compelled to turn from his
stony calmness to end her sorrows in the kinder
outstretched arms of dark night-waters; bitter
words to the woman watching her once-loved
husband slowly stepping downward to fill a drunk-
ard's grave; bitter words to the man who sees the
hard-earned savings of many toilsome years swept
away in one fell swoop at the beck of some re-

spected, mocking swindler; bitter, far more bitter
still, to the mother who sees her first-born son
struck low at her feet, made to lay down his life-
task scarce begun, and to yield his lusty vigor to
the grim silence of eternity ! These are the bitter
words that make a cynic of the maiden, a scoffer
of the man, and—God forgive us !—atheists of us
all in some despondent hour.   Yet whoever list-
ens long and earnestly to the deep-toned bell of
sorrow will hear at length a sweetness in its dying
tone, and will learn the key-note of the universe.
" Out of the strong cometh sweetness; out of the
sweetness, wisdom."

CHAPTER XVI.

No hope! No operation could save his life. Nothing could be done save to administer opiates to soothe his final struggles. Even the physicians—grave, quiet men so long familiar with every phase of suffering—showed their emotion by tearful eyes and unsteady voices as they walked away from the handsome, noble face and vigorous youthful frame so soon to be dismantled of its beauty. But one small consolation could they give—his faculties were gradually becoming deadened, and although he might linger for several hours in apparent agony, he would in reality become unconscious of his pain.

By the use of restoratives Philip again recovered consciousness. His first moaning words were: "The marriage must take place; it is all you can do for me; let me see them safely married. There is danger—danger, I say! Don't you know it? Hurry, I tell you! I will not die until you are married!" And he tried to raise himself from the pillows and to put out his hand to Flora. "And I want to see you in your wedding dress, too—" with a pitiful smile. The older of the two physicians, a genial, portly man, who had been a family friend of the McChesneys for many years, stepped forward and gently laid Philip back upon the pillows. "Everything shall be done as you wish, my child," said he, in soothing tones. "Do not waste your strength by any excitement. Trust it all to me."

Philip looked his gratitude as the physician said to Mr. McChesney: "There can be no reason why the ceremony should not take place now. It is, as Philip says, all that can be done for him. Let him see that his sister's future happiness will be assured. He, no doubt, feels that scruples will arise in both her mind and Signor Ferranti's which may end in their separation. Philip is the one to be considered, and let us all put aside every other feeling but his comfort. He very probably wishes that no more suffering than is necessary should result from this—" The physician spoke very calmly, but the evident difficulty of repressing his anger, as he sought for a word to characterize the dastardly crime that had been committed, caused his voice to suddenly break. He went up to Flora, whispered to her and led her to the foot of the stairs, where he gave her to kind old Margaret, with instructions to see that the half-fainting girl was dressed as quickly as possible in her wedding garments.

What a mockery seemed the array of finery

to Flora when entering the large sunny room she took in at one glance the still open trunks; the traveling dressing-case, with the tops of the bottles and backs of the brushes of tortoise-shell inlaid with gold; the silver and cut-glass toilet-sets; the white morocco writing-case, with gold monograms; and the glittering coronet shining out from its case of white satin and silver! Upon the bed beside the wedding dress, the bridal fan, one of Ferranti's gifts, was lying fully opened. It was of point lace and delicately carved ivory, the outer sticks incrusted with a lily-of-the-valley design in diamonds and small pearls; the lace opened in the center over three medallions surrounded with diamond sparks, the central medallion showing the Mantini coat-of-arms painted in water colors, above it a coronet in small diamonds; the other two medallions repeating the same design of Cupids upholding an exquisitely painted wreath of flowers, within which was Flora's monogram in tiny pearls. With a gesture of impatience, almost of contempt, Flora took up the fan, folded it, and then flung it back carelessly upon the bed. As it fell it struck one of the supports of the brass bedstead, and the dainty sticks of the almost priceless treasure snapped like glass. Old Margaret, instinctively following her habit of neatness, mechanically picked up a piece of ivory from the floor and put the fan together.

"Ah, dearie! ah, dearie!" she sighed, turning away to twist up Flora's disarranged hair.

Dressed finally in the wedding gown of soft satin and lace, and decked out with the diamond, opals, and pearls that formed the beautiful parure worn in turn by so many duchesses of Mantini, Flora sank in a melancholy heap upon the floor. "My strength has gone," she said; "I can not walk."

"Now, now, my bonny," said Margaret, picking her up and thrusting into her nerveless hands the bridal bouquet of pale orchids which harmonized with the faint flashes of color from her jewels, "they're waitin' now below; the young master maun have his gaze of the bride to cheer the wee bit moments of his life. Oh waes me it is, for the day he lies in the dust!" she moaned, while a tear trickled down her cheek and dropped on the white satin gown. "But there, there! I am an old fool. That's no way for us to be drappin' tears noo, and wailin' an' sighin' when 'tis time for work—an' the hardest kin' o' work—to smile when the heart is breakin'."

"Oh, but it is so cruel, so cruel! If it were not for me, this could not have happened." And Flora threw herself into the woman's arms.

"There, now; hush, hush," said Margaret, "'tis well I know nae ither mon can tak' the place o' that bonnie laddie, sae strang and sae leal. But ye canna help yoursel' lassie; you maun do as ye're bid and lift yoursel' aboon your dool. Ye maun put yoursel' awa', an' think to gladden his een with yer braw gown an' your jewels, and mak' him happy to see yer fast to yer ain gude man."

. Flora dashed her tears from her eyes, lifted her head from the broad shoulder of the woman, and, shutting her upper teeth over her under lip to still the nervous quiverings of the sensitive mouth, she went slowly down stairs and stood at the foot of Philip's couch.

"My good—my lovely darling!" whispered he, with a tender smile, "it is all right now. I can die in peace."

The clergyman had now arrived. After ad-minstering the Holy Communion to the dying man, he turned to join the living in the bonds that are more binding to the unhappy than the cerements of the grave. Ferranti's face was cold and stern and Flora's full of undefinable fear.

They stood at one end of the room, opposite the broad French window. The servants clustered near the doors; the physicians gathered in a knot at the head of the couch.

"Raise me in your arms, mother," whispered Philip with labored breath. And leaning on that breast which had pillowed his baby head—the breast whereon he had sobbed out his youthful grief, the mother-breast which is alike the refuge

of the child and the purest memory of the man—
Philip watched his sister's wedding.

The solemn closing words of the marriage service died away. Flora left her husband's side and
kissed her brother on cheeks, forehead, and lips.
"It was for you, Philip. I did this for you. I
can not be happy, now, without you. You know
that, don't you, darling? Oh, why, why, can I
not lie there instead of you!"

"Hush—you may not understand the will of
God. Time will show you that a few years are
but taken off a life that might have in it much
sin and sorrow. Don't think of my death. Flora
—mother, let all the pleasant memories of the past
cover the bitterness of our parting. You, Flora,
have a duty to your husband now; and mother
knows her own. She will bear up, as she always
has." Philip spoke with difficulty, but the broken
words were understood by those whose strained
attention was centered on the bluish, paling lips.
"You must go to Italy, and have mother go.
Take mother—my blessed, patient mother; she
will miss me—my mother will miss me," he murmured. "The place will be too sad for her just
yet." A wave of recollection seemed to sweep
over him, and he lifted himself suddenly, crying
out with renewed strength: "It is too hard! I
will not die! I can not—must not die! Life is
so fair, the world is so beautiful! And I am young

and strong! Is there no hope for me? no hope? I will not die! I am strong! Let me fight with death! O God! O God! It is too hard!" And he sank back panting on the pillows.

It was the final struggle of the unresigned flesh, of the body clinging to the spirit; the momentary cry wrung from the soul at loss of its earthly tenement—the cry that haunts forever those who hear it with its peal of ineffectual anguish.

"Forgive — forgive — this unmanliness," he said, as the choking sobs of his sister struck his ear. "Play to me—music will help me to be more calm."

"Philip," said Mr. McChesney, bending over him, "you said you knew the reason of this accident. If you do know, tell us. Give us, for heaven's sake, any clew you have to such villainy! Speak, my son, while you have strength."

Philip closed his eyes, and an expression of pain crossed his face. "Vengeance, vengeance, always vengeance," he muttered. "It is not for us to avenge ourselves, poor frail mortals steeped in sin! The man is already punished. He has overreached himself. His suffering and remorse begin with his knowledge of my death."

"Kalinski!" exclaimed Ferranti, stepping forward and clinching Mr. McChesney's arm with an iron grip.

"Stop!" said Philip. "The man is mine, to

punish or save, if I can. He shall have the
chance for atonement; and you," he said to Ferranti, "you I charge to help him carry it out. If
remorse does not kill him, give him my dying
command—to live my life as I would wish to live
it—and my forgiveness shall rest upon him, so
good may be born of evil. My charge, my dying
charge—" His voice failed as he looked appealingly
to Ferranti, and drops gathered on his forehead.
Unable to speak, he rested his anxious eyes upon
his mother. A violent paroxysm shook his frame.
His mother, every sense strained to the utmost to
anticipate his wish, motioned to Ferranti to get his
violin. Philip smiled faintly in his mother's face
as she wiped the cold dampness from his white
forehead, and he nodded when he heard the faint
tuning of the loved instrument. A passing gleam
of humor lit up the brown eyes. " Ferranti, a discord—the dominant seventh—no rest until it
meets the sweet harmony of a woman's nature—
together peace—the close—" These were the last
coherent words.

Ferranti began a minor strain of indescribable
sweetness. He bent his eyes upon Philip's face,
as though he would read each passing thought.
Master and violin were one. Never before had
the violin seemed so completely the voice of a
human soul struggling, aspiring, hoping, dream-
ing through the mazes of its earthly way. Mem-

ories of childhood, the brightness of the boy's un-
mixed delight, the glowing freedom of those hours
when quick blood courses in the veins and nature
is one vast storehouse of treasures unrevealed;
vague yearnings toward the spiritual good that
seems to flutter away from the soul's weak grasp,
burning resolutions to trample on all wrongs and
wake to fiery action the passive-moving world,
first rosy dreams of the ideal woman who flutters
vaguely through the youth's dim thought to take
firm outline in keener vision of the man; then
the pathos of disappointment, submission to the
inevitable, conquering sweetness of the spirit whispering content to the body tired of pain; rising
and falling in magic cadences these emotions swept
through the music's flowing tide as, borne away
upon the ocean, sweep a thousand shipwrecked
treasures to the shore. Now, like a shower of rain-
drops touched with sunlight, rippled out a farewell greeting to the sky, the trees, the mountains;
and now, woven together by pathetic chords, rolled
out in one shining web of melody a mingling of
strains from the great composers—strains associated in Philip's mind with the loves and friendships of his life. At the mother's favorite hymn,
which soared upward in clear, pure, and tremulous
notes from the violin, Philip looked at her with
one last gaze of unutterable affection. His labored
breathing had nearly ceased. The illumination

which irradiates the face of the dying at the final moment of dissolution, as if the soul smiled at parting from its earthly casing, overspread his face. Ferranti, with all the richness and fullness of tone at his command, broke into the andante from the Fifth Symphony which Philip had often played and which he had declared to be the most perfect musical expression of mingled sublimity and peace. Softer and softer grew each earnest note.

Then the last vibrations melted away in the low tones of the clergyman, who began to repeat the prayer for the dying. One fluttering sigh, and all was over. Ferranti dropped upon his knees. But the mother still held her son clasped closely to her breast. No sobs disturbed the stillness which followed ; no word was spoken until a yellow butterfly, lured by the perfume of the flowers gathered for the wedding, waveringly sailed through the open window and over Philip's couch. " It is the emblem of immortality," said the clergyman. "Thanks be to God who giveth us the victory, through Jesus Christ, our Lord. Amen."

.   .   .   .

The stars looked down throughout one warm spring night upon a motionless figure stretched upon a new-made grave. When the first bird notes began to herald the early dawn the man arose, his clothes damp with night dews, his eyes

11

bloodshot and wild with anguish. He cast a long, lingering glance over the fresh beauty of the peaceful scene. There was a quick flash—a dull report, and the figure again lay stretched upon the narrow grave, this time to rise no more.

So Emil Kalinski, according to his own ideas of justice, offered atonement for the life he had needlessly sacrificed. His hot and jealous rage had spent itself against the unanswerable fact of Philip's death as the simoon of the desert spends itself against the immovable Sphinx.

POSTLUDE.

The shadows of grief slowly passed away from Mr. and Mrs. McChesney. After returning from Italy, whither they had gone to accompany Flora to her new home, they settled by degrees to their usual duties and to renewed interest in their other children. Only now and then did they awake with a start to find that the memory of Philip was gradually being obscured by the clouding mists of every-day avocations. There is no keener pang to a sensitive heart than to recognize its own unfaithfulness to the sorrow it wedded with such ardor in the first moments of passionate despair. To such hearts it is long before the truth comes home that the greater faithfulness to the inner spirit of grief lies in an unselfish putting away of all that saddens the living. It is not forgetting, this putting away of grief into the holy, still recesses of memory, away from the noise and dust of day; rather is it the enshrinement of the dead in the precious amber of crystalized emotion.

Singularly, the weight of sorrow seemed to rest heaviest upon Flora. Even in her beautiful Italian home, adored by her husband and surrounded by the admiration of that aristocratic circle to which her husband's rank gave her entrance, she yet for several years bore about her the ethereal atmosphere that characterizes one to whom spiritual things are nearer than material. But she, too, is passing now to recognition of the fact that the needs of the living are greater than those of the dead. And the early passionate love for her husband, so jarred by the tragedy of her wedding day, is ripening to the fullness of its late fruition. She still accompanies him in the best old and new compositions for piano and violin, and on some rare evenings when the grand salons of the Mantini palace are thrown open to the dilettanti of Rome, artists and connoisseurs eagerly seize the opportunity to hear some great sonata rendered as it only can be rendered through the culture, intellect and sympathy of two such amateurs as the Duke of Mantini and his wife.

But the Duchess of Mantini will never play again the Rubinstein sonata, for she has learned

that it was the one best liked by the hapless Anita
and the most effective concert piece given by her
husband when, as Signor Ferranti, he appeared in
the concert halls of Paris.

THE END.